pigture
perfect

By Jenny Goebel

Scholastic Inc.

To my beloved grandmothers, Evelyn and Betty

1

Piglike dinosaurs called entelodonts roamed the earth approximately 16.3 million years ago.

When I saw the sticky note tucked in my stepdad's desk drawer, I felt a prickle of excitement. The note read: "Peak Veterinary Clinic." I'd found dozens of yellow sticky notes all over Mr. Pine's house since Mom and I had moved in. Some of his notes were reminders like "Change the furnace filter" or "Pick up laundry from the dry cleaners." Others were more random: the name of a series he wanted to watch on Netflix or the date of an upcoming meteor shower. However, not one of the other notes had been anywhere near as intriguing as this one.

My stepdad's sticky note obsession seemed slightly out of character considering he was such a neat freak. But Mom said organization wasn't the point of all his notes. She thought he developed the habit because he'd lived alone too long—which I found troubling. If things had been so boring that sticky notes had counted as conversation, well, it was no wonder I was causing such a disruption to his life. Mom thought it might help us get used to each other if I called him "Nathan" or "Dad," but since I couldn't see me or my stepdad ever feeling comfortable with that, I'd stuck with "Mr. Pine."

"Did you find one?" Mom's voice rang from down the hall and I sprang back. It felt like I'd been caught in the act, but I hadn't been snooping. Mom had sent me rummaging through my stepdad's desk in search of a red pen.

"Not yet," I called absently. My thoughts were still on the sticky note. There were no pets in the house, not even a goldfish, so why would Mr. Pine have the name of a vet written down? My heart thundered in my ears as I peeled back the first note and found a second one beneath: "Appointment— December 27, 11:00 a.m."

An appointment. At a veterinary clinic. Two days after Christmas. It could only mean one thing—I was finally getting a dog! In less than a week, there would be a cuddly four-legged companion waiting for me beneath the Christmas tree.

A squeal threatened to burst from my lungs, but I didn't want to ruin the surprise, and I didn't want to alarm Mr. Pine, who was sleeping right down the hall. I managed to swallow it back, but something like a whimper escaped my lips.

This was going to be the most spectacular, most amazing, most extraordinary Christmas ever. Not only was there snow in the forecast, for the first time in my life, Mom and I were living in a house instead of an apartment—which meant we had a yard. A *big*, canine-friendly yard. Mom's standard excuse for why we couldn't have a dog had been erased when she got married two months ago and we moved in with Mr. Pine. Unlike our cramped apartment, his larger home had a fence all the way around the property.

"Grace?" Mom's footsteps sounded on the hardwood right outside the office. I flipped the sticky notepad over and slid it back inside the drawer barely a second before Mom peeked her head around the corner and said, "Grace?" again.

I flashed her an unnatural smile.

Mom sized me up. She was dressed for work in a smart pantsuit and was holding a stack of holiday cards for all my teachers. She wanted the cards to have a festive feel—hence the need for a red pen. "Are you feeling all right?"

She stepped closer and placed a hand on my forehead. Her touch was warm and smooth. It quieted the bubbles fizzling inside me, and I felt my smile relax into something more normal. "I'm fine," I said. "Just anxious for winter break, that's all."

Mom nodded, clearly relieved. She glanced down at the

open drawer and fished out a blue ballpoint pen before ramming the drawer shut. "This will have to do." Then she quickly scribbled names on all the cards before handing me the stack. "You better get going. You'll miss the bus."

I took the cards, pecked her on the cheek, and bounded out of the room. Hopefully, she attributed the extra spring in my step to the fact that I was mere hours away from the freedom that came with winter break and didn't suspect that I'd uncovered the best Christmas surprise of my life.

Mom asked me to make a Christmas list every year. For the past seven years—ever since I learned to write—the number one thing on my list had been the same—a doodle dog. Labradoodle, Goldendoodle, Dalmadoodle, Sheepadoodle, Great Danoodle—I'd take any one of them. Really, I'd take any dog, but I knew a doodle dog would be hypoallergenic, and that was important because Mom had an intense sneezing reaction to anything with fur.

But this year, she hadn't asked me to make a list. I thought it was because she'd been too preoccupied with all the traveling she'd been doing since her big promotion at work. But the notes in Mr. Pine's desk drawer revealed the real reason. She hadn't needed me to. Mom already knew what I wanted.

Now that I'd uncovered the secret, it would kill me to hold it in until Christmas morning. I had to tell someone, and my best friend, Sydney, immediately sprang to mind. Most days, I didn't see her until lunchtime at school. Today, I needed to find her before first period. This was too important to wait.

I walked on air to the bus stop and was so fidgety while waiting that I might as well have been dancing. When the bus pulled up, I accidently made eye contact with Liam Rossi through one of the rectangular windows. He wiped away a thin layer of fog with his shirtsleeve, and his lips quirked into a goofy smile. I immediately felt self-conscious. Thankfully, it was only Liam who had witnessed my silly behavior. He was a little on the weird side, so I doubted he'd be one to judge me for acting strangely. Still, I reined in my Muppet arms and boarded at once.

I slid into my usual seat next to Jana. Unlike Liam, Jana was too wrapped up in her own anticipation to notice I could hardly sit still. Her family was traveling to New York City for the holidays. They had tickets for two Broadway shows and, "more importantly," to see the Rockettes in Radio City's *Christmas Spectacular.*

With Jana babbling about her trip, I managed to bottle up my own excitement for the entire bus ride. Really, it was for the best. Sydney would not be happy if I told Jana something this big before I told her.

As soon as the bus arrived at Riverbend Middle, I shot from

my seat and raced down the sidewalk and through the glass doors. Once inside, I immediately began scanning for my best friend. I hated not being able to walk to school with her now that I rode the bus.

Last year, when Sydney and I were in fifth grade at Riverbend Elementary, we were both in the same homeroom and we hardly spent a moment apart all day long. Now that we were in middle school, we only had two classes together. They were both in the afternoon. The first day of middle school had been sheer misery when I realized I wouldn't see her all morning. Three different elementary schools fed into Riverbend Middle. So, many of the faces in my classes had been new. I didn't automatically have the status of being Sydney's best friend. And the students I didn't know, even some of the teachers, had treated me differently. My jokes weren't as funny; at least I didn't get the same responses. When I spoke, no one seemed to care what I had to say. Nobody was clamoring to be with me for group work. Without Sydney, I wasn't as bright or smart or worthy.

Apparently, luck was still on my side. Right away, I spotted Sydney at the end of the main hallway. She was hard to miss. She was beautiful, in a glowing, fresh-faced sort of way—the kind of pretty that adults especially seemed to cherish. Even her posture made her stand out. Just about everyone in middle school had slouching issues, myself included. Not Sydney, though. Her head was always high, and her shoulders were back, like she assumed she was being watched. Which, most of the time, she was. With her sleek chestnut-colored hair, graceful movements, and pretty face, she was always turning heads.

A few more minutes and the hallway would be too packed to reach her. I took off sprinting, dodging bodies left and right as I went. When she started to move around the corner and out of sight, I loudly yelled, "Sydney!" She spun and then froze with an unreadable expression on her face. No matter—I knew she'd be thrilled when I told her the good news. But with just a few short steps left, Mr. Houshmand moved his hulking body between us. I was forced to come skidding to a stop.

"There's no running or yelling in the halls, young lady," he scolded. I knew this. I also knew that breaking not one but two rules could get me written up and result in an email being sent home—a thought that deflated my excitement faster than a withering balloon.

Sydney scooted around Mr. Houshmand and looped an arm through mine. "We're sorry," she interjected sweetly. Sydney was every teacher's dream. She was super composed and respectful, not to mention that she always earned straight As.

I felt the instant boost of having my best friend beside me. And the thing about Sydney was that some of her glow naturally radiated to those around her.

The expression on Mr. Houshmand's face softened into an almost smile.

"Grace would never break the hall rules unless it was important," Sydney said. "Right, Grace?"

I nodded, but my head must've bounced up and down a tad too enthusiastically. A look of displeasure flickered in Sydney's eyes before she once again shone her benevolent smile upon the teacher.

For a millisecond, doubt clouded his expression, like he suspected he was being played. But it wasn't enough to challenge Riverbend Middle's most darling student. He tipped his head in silent dismissal.

I breathed a sigh of relief while Sydney guided me around the corner. "What was that all about?" she whispered.

After having the news bottled up for so long, it came gushing out. "I'm getting a dog! I found a note this morning in my stepdad's desk and it had the name of a veterinary clinic and an appointment time for December 27, and I know, I just know, I'm getting a dog for Christmas this year!" I grabbed one of Sydney's arms while I bounced up and down.

"Grace, you're talking too loudly," Sydney said through a plastered-on smile. "Mr. Houshmand is going to come back."

"Oh, right," I said, lowering my voice. Then I dropped

Sydney's arm and stopped bouncing on my feet. Still, my left foot jiggled a little. I couldn't help it.

My best friend never lost her composure. She was a gentle breeze while I brought gale-force winds. She was a soft sunbeam while I was a blinding light. It had been that way forever. Sydney's mom had provided childcare for me while Mom was finishing college and starting her career. Sydney and I were so different that sometimes I worried the only reason we were friends was because we'd practically grown up together.

Unlike Sydney, I hadn't been an easy child. I was noisy and disruptive—laughter, tears, or rage—whatever I was feeling, everyone knew about it. Mom never came right out and said it, but I knew I'd been a lot of work. She didn't have much time or energy left for anything or anyone else. Eventually, I learned to control my outbursts but not before Dad left. Sometimes I wondered if he might've stayed if I'd been more like Sydney.

"A dog is nice . . ." Sydney said, "but what happened to getting a phone?"

I refused to feel deflated by Sydney's response. Of course she'd think a phone was more important. She wanted me to have a phone like she did, so we wouldn't always have to communicate through our moms. Plus, she already had a golden retriever.

"It's . . . complicated," I said. I'd asked for a phone for my birthday, but my stepdad had talked Mom into giving me a

Polaroid camera instead. He didn't think a phone was appropriate for someone my age. And even though Sydney wouldn't understand, I didn't feel comfortable arguing with Mr. Pine about it. Things between me and my stepdad were strained enough. I didn't need any more strikes against me.

Sydney let out a note of disappointment. Then her eyes landed on something, make that *someone*, standing behind me. Her expression hardened. "What do *you* want?"

I turned, and there was Liam Rossi. My eyes were immediately drawn to his bright green "Eat Bugs, Save the Planet" T-shirt. I wondered if he was serious about that. Probably. Unlike most boys, his insect obsession had lasted way past third grade. He was also the type of boy that Sydney tsk-tsked for wearing pants that were too short and for showing up at school with hair that was shaggy and never styled.

I was afraid he would ask why I'd been dancing at the bus stop and reveal my silly behavior to Sydney. Instead he held out a white envelope. I immediately recognized Mom's neat handwriting (in blue ink instead of red).

"This fell out of your backpack," Liam said. "I tried to catch you, but you took off too fast."

"Oh, thank you!" And then, because it was true, and because I wanted to say something nice in return for his thoughtful action, I added, "I like your photographs."

The photography club had lined one of the school hallways with blown-up photographs they'd taken throughout the semester. There were nature scenes, self-portraits, and some dramatic black-and-whites. Liam's photos appeared to be normal everyday things. But in each photo, a random item had been replaced with something made from Legos. One had a fruit bowl with a banana and some oranges, and then a single redbrick apple. Another photo was taken in a garden with real flowers, real plants, real rocks, and then a Lego praying mantis.

His photographs were a bit odd, like Liam himself, but something about them made me smile. They made all the other photographs seem like they were trying too hard. And even though Liam was inserting something imaginary into each one, his felt more authentic than the rest. Like he was doing something that amused him instead of aiming to snap a prizewinning photograph.

"Maybe you should join the photography club," he offered.

I shifted my weight from one foot to the other. I'd asked Sydney to join the photography club with me at the beginning of the school year. Sydney loved art, so naturally, I thought she'd like it. At first, she seemed interested, but then she saw the names on the sign-up list and changed her mind. And I hadn't wanted to do it without her.

Sydney spoke up before I could answer. "We were in the

middle of a conversation," she said in the same sweet voice she'd used with Mr. Houshmand. "So if you don't mind . . ."

"Oh, right," Liam said bashfully. "Sorry." He shuffled away and was swallowed up by the flood of students now pouring into the hallway.

"Anyway, we should go to class, but I'm really happy for you," Sydney said, and gave me a quick hug. "I didn't mean to make you feel badly about the phone. I just wanted to be able to talk to you more over break. But a puppy will be super fun."

My insides started humming again, and I was back to feeling on top of the world. "Thanks, Syd," I said, forgetting all about Liam and the photography club. "I can't wait for Christmas."

2

The average weight of a domestic pig is between 300 and 1,000 pounds. The world record for the heaviest pig is held by Big Bill. Big Bill weighed in at a whopping 2,552 pounds.

Over the next few days, my excitement grew as I pictured all the fun things I would do with my new pet. We'd go on walks and play fetch and curl up together to watch movies. It probably goes without saying, but when Christmas morning rolled around, I woke up bright and early. It didn't matter in the slightest that it'd taken me forever to fall asleep. My brain had been super active the night before. Images of soft, wet noses, sweet floppy ears, and wagging tails kept flooding my mind. So even though my eyes hadn't been shut all that long, they popped open at precisely 5:12 a.m. The second they did, the images came rushing back.

The wait was torturous. Still, I knew better than to leave my room before 6:00 a.m. Mom would *want* to kill me for getting up before the crack of dawn, but I knew she'd forgive me. Mr. Pine might not. So I watched the time creep by on my alarm clock and took deep breaths so my heart wouldn't explode when I thought of all the sweet, fluffy snuggles in my near future.

Forty-eight painfully long minutes later I bounded down the hallway. I ran straight for the Christmas tree in the front room. The three stockings strung above the fireplace were bulging, but the space beneath the tree was pretty bare. The presents I'd wrapped were there—a tablet pillow stand for Mom and socks for Mr. Pine. But only a few others.

Of course, I'd been hoping to find my dog first thing. And on any other Christmas, I might've been disappointed by the lack of presents, but this year it only made it seem more likely that my suspicions were correct. Then there was the large bag in the garage. It appeared the day after I'd discovered the note. Mr. Pine had covered it with a blanket, so none of the print was visible, but what else came in a bag that size, shape, and material other than dog food? Also, I'd seen Mr. Pine walking the perimeter of the backyard fence on December 23. Obviously he'd been looking for holes a puppy could wriggle through. It all added up to me being one hundred percent certain that my dreams were about to come true.

What I didn't know was how my dog would be presented.

Was he in a box hidden somewhere? Would Mom lead him out with a bow around his neck?

Mom and Mr. Pine were usually straightforward in their delivery of things. I hoped they wouldn't choose this Christmas to get creative. My heart couldn't bear a drawn-out scavenger hunt, or any other sort of trickery. It felt like I'd waited my entire life for this day to come, and now that it was here, I thought I'd burst if I had to wait a minute longer.

I bounced on my toes and jiggled the way I had at the bus stop the day before break started. If it were just Mom and me, I'd race to her room and wake her. But things were different now. So I switched from bouncing to pacing back and forth. I didn't lighten my steps any, though. If anything, they were heavier than usual as I paraded across the wooden floor.

The thought of even louder footsteps struck me as a brilliant idea, and I dug my snow boots from the closet. There was snow in the forecast, after all; who could blame me for being prepared?

I slipped them on and stomped a few steps down the hallway before having second thoughts. One of the few things I remembered about my dad was how angry he would get when I would "wake the whole neighborhood" on a weekend morning.

When I heard a door creak open, I yanked my feet free of the boots and tiptoed back to the living room. Seconds later, a loud crash, followed by a swear word, echoed down the hallway. Then Mr. Pine appeared carrying my boots. "Are these yours, Grace?" he asked.

Clearly they couldn't belong to anyone else, but I nodded just the same.

"I'd appreciate it if you didn't leave them lying around for people to trip on," my stepdad said tersely.

"I'm sorry," I said.

One side of his mouth lifted. "It's all right, and, um . . . merry Christmas."

It shouldn't have felt awkward. He and Mom had dated for a year before they'd married. Mom had wanted me to get to know him before they ever got "serious." What I'd learned was that he was nice (not all Mom's boyfriends had been) and he was patient (again, not all Mom's boyfriends had been). But we never seemed to know what to say to each other. So whenever we wound up alone, it was like we were both looking for a way to escape.

"Thanks," I said. I took the boots from his hands and peered down the empty hallway behind him.

"Your mom will be out soon," he added. "She's in the bathroom." Mr. Pine went to the window and pulled back the curtain, revealing a dull brown-and-gray world outside. "So much for snow," he said, his disappointment obvious.

I fidgeted. I wanted a white Christmas, too. But our first Christmas as a family could still be perfect without snow, couldn't it?

"Good morning!" Mom was wearing her plush cream-colored bathrobe. As she swept me into a hug, I felt her lips brush the top of my head and I smelled the fresh-scented hand lotion she applied every morning.

I hugged her back, then gazed longingly at the tree. "Can we?" I asked. I wasn't sure if there was a new protocol. Mom and I had our own Christmas-morning traditions. We had matching snowman-shaped mugs from which we drank hot chocolate while we sorted the presents into two piles, and then we took turns opening them one by one. But I knew, like everything else, that Mom would want our customs to mix together with Mr. Pine's. Or at least that's what she'd say, "mix together." Still it felt like we were making most of the changes. We'd moved into his house and taken his last name.

"Well, I thought we'd start with breakfast this year," she said.

I forced myself to smile. "Sure," I said. "Breakfast." No matter that Mom and I had always drunk so much hot chocolate on Christmas morning that we hadn't had room for anything else. Sydney's family always ate a French toast casserole and eggs and a berry salad for Christmas breakfast. So maybe that's what families were supposed to do—have breakfast together *before* presents.

We started toward the kitchen, when Mom halted in her tracks and said, "Oh! There is one present that can't wait until after we eat . . . Stay right here."

I held my breath while Mom raced back to her bedroom. I thought, *This is it.* She was going to emerge with my dog. I just knew it. With a dog sitting on my lap, or by my feet, I knew I could endure any length of meal.

But the gift Mom returned with was too small to contain any sort of doodle dog. It was too small to even contain a Chihuahua. "Here," Mom said, and pushed the present into Mr. Pine's hands. "I thought you should have this."

The gift turned out to be a snowman mug—not identical to the ones Mom and I owned but close enough. Mom and Mr. Pine got all mushy for a second, and I turned my head.

"Now we're ready for breakfast *and* hot chocolate," Mom said.

Not only did I have to sit through a meal before presents, I had to sit through Mr. Pine and Mom cooking it. Mom scrambled eggs and toasted wheat bread. Mr. Pine chopped potatoes into tiny chunks to panfry on the stove, which took forever. I mean, what's wrong with frozen hash browns? I bit my tongue so my impatience would stay trapped inside me. My knees

that she'd brought presents. I felt a rush of panic. It hadn't occurred to me to buy her anything. Then I noticed that her eyes were puffy, like she'd been crying. And the bags I'd thought were presents were really duffel bags and suitcases—a whole bunch of them. It appeared she'd brought with her every item of clothing she owned.

"I don't understand," Mr. Pine was saying as I approached.

"What don't you understand?" she said dryly. "I'm moving in."

My stomach lurched, and I exchanged a glance with Mom, who was standing at the back of the room, allowing Mr. Pine to handle the situation. Her shoulders lifted, almost imperceptibly in a shrug.

"Today? On Christmas?" Mr. Pine asked.

"It's not like I have a choice. I mean, I do, but this is literally my best option. Trust me, I wouldn't be here if it wasn't." She looked around, taking in our surprise. "Mom didn't tell you? She said she would call, but I guess she had more *important* things on her mind." Emma couldn't hide the pain in her voice, and I felt a flicker of sympathy for her. Not enough to overcome my unease about her moving in, though.

I was so caught up in the drama unfolding before me that the pig was momentarily pushed to the back of my mind. That was until a large pinkish squealing blur came barreling through the room and out the open door. Mom gasped. Mr. Pine bellowed, "Oh nooo."

Eyes wide, Emma jumped out of the way as the rest of us darted after the pig.

I groaned as I went, realizing that I'd left the door to the garage open when I'd come into the front room to investigate. I'd had no idea I'd be giving the pig a straight shot at escape. He made it as far as the front yard before stopping in the middle of it, as if he'd been expecting to find something else. More pigs? A giant mud puddle? Who knew?

My stepdad, who arrived on the lawn a few steps ahead of Mom and me, shouted at the animal, "Here, pig!" When the pig made unhappy grunts and didn't move any closer, Mr. Pine laughed uncomfortably and shook his head. "The rescue said pigs are a little wary of new situations. He doesn't know any of us well enough yet, or I'm sure he'd come when called."

Mr. Pine crept toward the pig, crouching low and spreading out his arms. Mom circled behind him and approached slowly. I positioned myself halfway between them so that we more or less formed a triangle around the pig.

When Mr. Pine nodded his head, all three of us lunged.

The pig squealed again. Then he shot straight between Mr. Pine's legs. My stepdad nearly folded over on top of himself trying to stop the wild animal. Mom and I sprang into action.

It was fortunate that the snow hadn't materialized. Otherwise, we would've been sliding all over the place as we raced around, repetitively trying and failing to contain the pig.

It must've been a sight to see. Mom in her bathrobe making oinking noises, no doubt attempting to communicate to the pig that he shouldn't fear us. And Mr. Pine in his flannel pajamas, waving his arms wildly about. When making exaggerated gestures didn't work, he changed tactics and began talking softly. "It's all right, pig. We won't hurt you. Come back inside."

At least I'd thought to get dressed when I'd jumped out of bed that morning, but that didn't make the situation any less embarrassing. What would the neighbors think? How had a Christmas that had seemed so promising when I'd awoken gone so disastrously wrong? I covered my eyes. I could scarcely bear to watch anymore.

When I peeked, I saw Emma emerging from the house, holding the plate of kitchen scraps Mr. Pine had made us save. "Come here, pig," she said soothingly, and lowered the plate to the concrete stoop. The pig wiggled the flat disk nose in the center of his face and considered. But not for long. He trotted right up to her and buried his snout in the plate.

"Good boy," Emma said, and took half a step backward, then another and another—bringing the plate and, therefore, the pig with her. Inch by inch she lured him back inside the house.

As I took the rear following everyone back inside, I was struck with a thought that added another layer of worry to my anxiety. I knew Mr. Pine had been lonely living in an empty home before Mom and I moved in. Mom had said so. But now an animal had been added to the household and his daughter was moving back in. It had gone from just him to four people and a pig in a matter of months. That was a big change for someone who liked peace and order, and I experienced a vague feeling of dread as I walked into a house that was far noisier and more crowded than it had been in years.

4

The most common type of miniature pig is a potbellied pig, which has an average weight of 70 to 150 pounds.

After returning the pig to the garage, we reconvened in the kitchen. "I can't believe you gave *her* a pig," Emma said in a small, whiny voice. "Not to mention my room."

I wanted to tell her that I didn't even want the pig. That what I wanted was to send him back to where he came from and that I hadn't known it was her room. But I knew staying quiet was a better option. If I made a fuss, I'd only make myself seem like more of a nuisance.

Mr. Pine cleared his throat and said, "It hasn't been your room for over a decade. How was I supposed to know you'd be moving back in?"

"Emma, it might help if you explained *why* you're moving back in," Mom said. I knew the various tones of Mom's voice well enough to know that all she was doing was getting to the heart of the matter. She didn't mean to sound so forward. That's just the way she was. Mom was a problem solver. It's why she was so good at her job as a business consultant. It made me squirm a little, though. I still felt like an outsider, like we shouldn't butt into Mr. Pine and his daughter's business. Obviously, Mom didn't share my opinion.

Mr. Pine and Emma were standing by the kitchen counter. Mom and I sat at the breakfast nook—out of the way, but not as far removed from the tension as I wanted to be. I listened quietly while Emma explained how her Mom's boyfriend had proposed the night before. He'd dropped to one knee in front of their Christmas tree and presented a ring. It sounded romantic to me. But the way Emma told it—with eye rolls and huffs of disgust—it was clear she saw things differently.

"Mom said with Grams gone, there's nothing to keep her here anymore and she's moving to Arizona to be with him. Nothing here?" Emma's voice went from sounding whiny to wheezy and constricted. "What about me? She doesn't seem to care that I only have one semester of high school left. *One.* I can't pack up and leave now. But apparently, she's not willing to put her life on hold for me any longer. With or without me, she said she's going."

"So I'm guessing it's without," Mr. Pine said wryly, even though it was the wrong time for a joke.

Mom winced, and I shifted closer to the wall, wishing it was a door.

Emma glanced at the three matching half-empty mugs of hot chocolate where we'd left them on the kitchen counter. Tears pooled in the corners of her eyes, but she didn't cry. And she didn't comment on the mugs. Still, I thought I recognized her sadness. She had to feel displaced. Her mom was leaving, and strangers had moved into her dad's house. I felt sorry for her. But it wasn't like I could fix her situation. I supposed I could sleep on the couch, and she could have my room—er, I mean her room—back.

Emma's eyes drifted from the mugs to the garage door, and she redirected the conversation back to the pig. "How many times did I beg you for a pig before you and Mom split?" she said wistfully.

I felt something turn over in the pit of my stomach. Is that why Mr. Pine had rescued the pig? Is that why he thought *all* kids wanted one? I was growing more uncomfortable by the minute. A pig didn't seem like the best fit for keeping an immaculate home. But if he was trying to do something for me that he wished he'd done for his daughter, it made more sense.

Why couldn't he have just gone with a dog? I hadn't figured

out my place in this new family yet, and a dog would've really helped. I would've had a companion—a furry friend to walk on a leash and snuggle up with during family movie nights. That way, Mom wouldn't always have to divide her attention between me and Mr. Pine.

As it was, she always got squashed between us when we crowded together on the couch. Worse, when we went on walks, the sidewalk wasn't wide enough for three people. So Mom would walk holding hands with my stepdad for a bit and then fall back a step so she could walk beside me. Mr. Pine didn't act like it bugged him, but how could it not?

Now, though, instead of a dog, I had a pig I didn't want, and a stepsister who'd wanted a pig but never had one. Things felt more jumbled up and uneven than ever.

"Mom, should I go check on the pig?" I whispered, and tipped my head toward the garage. It was pretty much the last thing I wanted—I'd much rather have gone to my room, only I wasn't sure it was my room now that Emma was moving back in. All I knew was it was too cold to be outside but that I needed to get out of the kitchen.

Mom nodded. I could see in her eyes that this wasn't the way she'd imagined our first Pine family Christmas going either.

I quietly slipped into the garage. After pulling the door

shut behind me, I collapsed onto the wooden step. Which apparently was enough to force the pig back into the far corner. He still wanted nothing to do with me. I sighed, then let my gaze drift to the bag of chow that up until this morning had been covered by a blanket. I'd assumed it was dog food. Now that it was exposed, I could see the hefty pig pictured on the front. The food, the note about the veterinarian, the empty space beneath the tree—I'd been so certain they were all signs pointing to a dog. Instead, my Christmas had been upended by a pig.

I turned my attention back to the hulking pink animal in the corner. He wasn't a piglet, but he wasn't as plump and large as the model pig on the food bag either. It was almost comical the way his weight was supported by dainty little hooves. And even though he was mostly pink, he had a few dark patches of hair and a kidney-shaped black spot behind his left ear.

The longer I sat there, the more he seemed to be relaxing. He ventured a little way out of the corner and began exploring the garage. As he sniffed around with a snout that took up an entire third of his face, his hooves clicked and clacked on the cement. When he came upon a crumpled-up newspaper next to the trash bin, he grunted happily and wagged his tail.

He pushed the newspaper ball with his snout, seemingly delighted to have something to play with. It made me want a dog even more. The wagging tail, the playfulness—it was just similar enough to remind me of what I was missing.

It made me heartsick knowing I either had to accept that I wasn't getting a dog, or I had to march back into the kitchen and cause another disruption. Considering what Emma was going through, though, complaining about a Christmas present seemed selfish. Plus, I didn't want to hurt Mr. Pine's feelings. That meant I had to make the most of a bad situation. I had to pretend I was happy with the pig. I would try my hardest to be gracious and appreciative. Really, it wasn't much different than a dog. It was about the same size. It had that wagging tail.

I had an idea. I sprang from the step and rummaged through an overhead cabinet until I found what I was looking for. If the pig liked the crumpled newspaper, I thought he would love a tennis ball.

"Fetch!" I yelled, and gently tossed the ball across the garage. It bounced across the floor and rolled to a stop near the pig's hooves. He snorted, then snuffled the ball around with his snout. He did not pick it up. He certainly did not return it to me.

"Here, pig. Come here, pig," I called just as the door creaked open behind me.

"It might help if you gave him a name," Emma said. She

looked down her nose at me, and the diamond stud sparkled in the light. "Just a thought."

I clenched my fists and summoned a smile. "Okay, thanks," I said.

"Look, my dad wanted me to tell you that you can keep the room. He's moving his desk to the basement and I'm taking the office."

I felt a smidge of relief. This was good news, wasn't it? Emma was the one displacing him, not me. At least, I hoped he'd see it that way.

Emma hugged herself and ran her hands up and down her bare arms. "Brrrr. The garage is cold. You know, pigs don't have a lot of hair to keep them warm. You should probably bring him inside."

"Right." Despite my sour feelings toward the pig, he couldn't help that he wasn't a dog. And I didn't want him to freeze out here. But I had no idea how I was supposed to move him.

Emma stared at me pointedly like she was waiting for me to do something. I knew the pig wasn't going to come on command, so I walked over to him. Seventy-five pounds wasn't *that* heavy. I'd picked up Sydney before and carried her a few feet across the school playground, and she probably weighed more than the pig. Bending my knees, I dropped down to his level, wrapped my arms underneath his belly, and then lifted.

"SqueeeeeeeSqueeeeeee!" The pig let out the most blood-curdling murder squeal I'd ever heard. I set him down immediately.

"Are you ever going to learn?" Emma asked before ripping into the bag of pig chow. She scooped out a handful. Then she proceeded to make a trail of pig pellets, Hansel-and-Gretel style, leading up the wooden steps and into the kitchen.

The pig greedily gobbled up the pellets one by one as he trotted right inside. Chagrined, I followed a step behind his wagging tail.

"Well, what about that name?" Emma asked.

I hesitated. I hadn't had any intention of naming the pig, but I wanted to show Emma that I could be pleasant and easygoing. I wanted her to see that I was trying hard to make the best of our new living situation. "Bernard." Then, with more conviction, I said, "The pig's name is Bernard. You know, like a Saint Bernard."

She scowled. "Bernard sounds like an old man's name. Why not Wilbur, or Mercy, or Hamlet, or Pumbaa, or Babe, or Poppleton, or Porky? Even Porky would be better than Bernard."

So much for making the best of things. I squared my shoulders and took a deep breath. Keeping my cool around her was already proving difficult. "His name is Bernard," I said as stoically as I could. Then I walked past her and into the house on the heels—make that hooves—of the pig.

5

Miniature potbellied pigs are descendants of Vietnamese potbellied pigs, which were first imported to the United States in the 1980s.

While Mom and Mr. Pine emptied the office of furniture and moved a daybed up from the basement, I hung out with Bernard. He must've been exhausted from going all, er, hog wild on the front lawn that morning. He went straight to one corner of my room, dropped to the floor, then shut his eyes.

Flopped over on one side and with his legs sprawled outward, he fell asleep, his mouth curled into a smile. *What do pigs dream about?* I wondered. As the round disk in the middle of his face began to wiggle to and fro and he smacked his lips together, I thought, *Oh, right, food.*

In addition to the bag of pig chow, Mr. Pine had brought home a giant litter box, a leash, a harness, and food and water bowls. Fortunately, as evidenced by a deposit in the litter box, Bernard was already house-trained. Or so I thought.

Curious how Emma's room was progressing, I wandered out of my room and down the hallway to peek at what everyone else was up to. Emma was unpacking her bags into a chest of drawers, and Mom and my stepdad were loading file folders into boxes to be carried to the basement. I stayed quiet and out of the way, but I wondered if this was how any of them had envisioned spending what was supposed to be a really special day.

At least wonderful smells were wafting down the hallway from the kitchen. Mom and I had always skimped on Christmas breakfast but not dinner. Dinner would be a feast, followed by dessert. My mouth began to water just thinking about the pineapple upside-down cake with brown sugar and maraschino cherries. Mom only made it once a year—on Christmas. And her mother and her mother's mother made it before her. It was a tradition—one of ours, not Mr. Pine's. And from the smell of things, Mom had baked it early, before dinner.

Something about pineapple and warm cake was like a whiff of spring air in the dead of winter. With the comforting smell of my favorite dessert, the pig napping, and Emma getting settled in, it felt like we'd turned a corner. Like life was getting back on track. Maybe Christmas wasn't a total loss after all. And the glue between me and Mom and Mr. Pine wasn't dry yet, so maybe a reconfiguration wasn't out of the question. Maybe we could go from a family of three to a family of four—well, five counting Bernard—without any more mishaps.

A loud crash rang out from the kitchen, and then another. Mom glanced from me to Emma to Mr. Pine and looked bewildered. We were all here. Who could be making such a ruckus? Then her gaze shot back to me, and I think it hit us both at the same time.

She sprang to her feet as I groaned, "Oh no."

"The pig," we said in unison.

The four of us raced to the kitchen. The mess we found was breathtaking.

My stomach plummeted. Mom and Mr. Pine both gasped. Emma snickered, then said, "Oh my hog."

The lacey tablecloth was on the floor. The fancy silverware Mom only put out on Christmas was strewn across the kitchen, as well as a toppled cake platter and several other dishes. The pineapple upside-down cake was right side up near the base of the table, and Bernard had his face buried in it—gleefully rooting around in the spongy cake and slurping up cherries and pineapple slices to his heart's content. In short, he was in hog heaven.

All I could figure was that to retrieve his prize, Bernard had latched on to the cloth and tugged it to the floor along with everything else that had been resting upon the table.

Uh-oh. What would Mr. Pine think of this mess? Granted,

he'd brought the pig home, but Bernard was my pet now. My responsibility.

Mom reeled on my stepdad. "I *thought* you said the pig was house-trained." The clip in her voice pushed a dusty button somewhere deep inside me. I didn't want Mom to argue with Mr. Pine like she used to fight with my biological father.

So I was relieved when he said calmly, "I suppose litter-trained is not the same as house-trained and I failed to distinguish between the two." At least he wasn't blaming me for Bernard's transgressions. *Yet.* I'd have to be more careful in the future.

Mom shot Mr. Pine a withering look, then said, "Well, thank goodness we still have ice cream."

The thing about the ice cream was that Mr. Pine had purchased it. Mom knew the value of delicious, creamy ice cream made with real vanilla. When it came to grocery shopping, however, Mr. Pine shopped by price alone. Therefore, the freezer was stocked with not one but four off-brand cartons because there had been a buy-one-get-one-free special and Mr. Pine could "never pass up a bargain."

I quickly began to gather the forks and spoons strewn around the kitchen floor. As much as I wanted to openly mourn the loss of the upside-down cake, I could not. If I acted like it wasn't a big deal that dessert was ruined, then maybe no one else would care either. Maybe the day could still be salvaged.

But despite my efforts, the disappointments kept on coming.

The feast Mom had planned on for Christmas dinner centered around a ham. A ham! Either this hadn't been communicated to Mr. Pine before he decided a living pig would be the perfect surprise gift, or else he hadn't put two and two together.

Neither did Mom, apparently, until after we'd tidied up and she pulled it from the fridge to start preparing dinner. Emma took one look at the honey-baked ham with the red foil wrapping and balked. "You can't be serious."

"What?" Mom asked. Then closed her eyes and gravely said, "Oh."

That's how we ended up eating cold leftover pizza and freezer-burned generic ice cream on Christmas. While we ate, Mr. Pine chewed his pizza crust thoughtfully. "It's probably best if the pig remains outside, or in the garage when unsupervised from here on out," he said. "I'll add an overhead heater for when it gets cold. But don't worry, Grace, he can sleep in your room at night."

"Um, thanks," I said, then added, "I can't wait," and I tried to sound like I meant it.

Emma set her pizza slice down. "I'm not hungry," she said.

I removed a piece of Canadian bacon from my own, then picked off an olive and ate it.

Later that night, Mom delivered an armful of blankets to my room along with my stocking. In all the excitement, we'd never gotten around to opening them. It seemed like it'd been a hundred years since I'd run out of my room that morning, certain that what lay ahead was the best day of my life.

With a heavy sigh, I thanked her and took the stocking from her hands. Peeking inside, I could see tubes of my favorite lip gloss, lotion, and bath bombs.

"I did *some* of the Christmas shopping," she said. "I regret not doing all of it."

I helped her pile the blankets in the corner. No sooner had we set them down than Mr. Pine was ushering Bernard into my room. As quickly as he'd popped in, my stepfather was off to Emma's room to say good night.

Mom lingered in my doorway while Bernard rooted around in the bed of blankets, pushing his snout under and through until he'd woven himself into the pile. When he'd finished, his eyes were hidden beneath a fuzzy red throw. Guessing by the way he suddenly went still, he'd dozed off in a matter of seconds.

"Well," said Mom.

"Well," I said, then added, "At least you haven't sneezed once all day."

"Nope. Nathan was right about that. The pig does seem to be hypoallergenic. Whereas an actual Saint Bernard . . ." Mom trailed off as she cast me a sad smile. "Look, Grace, I know this isn't the pet you had your heart set on," she said. "But we're in the thick of things now. Do you think you can live with it?"

I put on a brave face because I knew it's what she wanted me to do. Since marrying Mr. Pine, she didn't seem exhausted all the time and she didn't stress out over little things like paying the utility bill. These days, she smiled for no reason and laughed even when a joke wasn't all that funny. It was obvious how happy Mr. Pine and our new life made her, and I knew she wanted me to be happy, too. For the most part, I was. The last thing I wanted was for me or my pig to mess it all up.

Before the wedding, Mom had said, "Anytime you blend businesses, people, or families together, there are going to be bumps in the road. Nobody should have to give up their dreams, or lose sight of who they are, but there are going to be sacrifices and compromises all around. It's the only way it can work."

At the time, I'd been upset about moving away from Sydney. I was doing my best to swallow the changes as they came. Now I tried to think of Bernard as another bump in the road. A compromise. He wasn't a dog, but how different could the two be? There wasn't any reason I couldn't treat him the same way I would a puppy. He was still a pet, just like a dog, and pets were commonly found in healthy families. I could live with a pet pig. How hard could it be?

6

Miniature pigs continue to grow until the age of five, making it difficult to know how large a piglet will be as an adult.

I let out a shriek when I felt Bernard's flat snout press against the sole of my foot. One of my legs had wriggled free from the comforter while I slept. Apparently, Bernard had decided to investigate. I recoiled at once and drew both legs to my chest. In the dim light, I could barely make out the pig's substantial form in the darkness.

He grunted, then wandered back over to his pile of blankets and collapsed on the heap. It was the first time he'd come near me by choice, and I wasn't sure what to make of it. I mean, it wasn't a pleasant experience—having a warmish, flat nose unexpectedly connect with my foot in the middle of the night. But I hoped it meant that he was growing more comfortable around me. In order to make the most of the situation, the two of us would have to get used to each other.

I stretched out flat again and closed my eyes. When I woke the next morning, Bernard was sprawled out on a blanket. Not in the corner where I'd last seen him, but on the floor at the foot of my bed. A whoosh of letdown escaped my lungs. I was disappointed all over again. How many times had I longed for a fluffy doodle dog curled up close to me while I slept at night? This plump, snoring beast was not the same.

The edges of my curtains glowed. I quietly stepped over the pig and drew them back, flooding the room with soft morning light. The gray skies had teased with the promise of snow all Christmas Day, but this morning there wasn't a cloud in the sky.

Okay, I thought. *I can do this. Today, I will take Bernard for a walk.* I figured getting us both out of the house would be the easiest way to avoid a repeat of yesterday's kitchen catastrophe. It was a trick I'd learned when I was little. Making myself scarce had been a sure way to reduce tension between my mom and my biological dad. Surprisingly, my stepdad hadn't come unglued about the mess, but I knew it was only a matter of time before his patience wore thin. I only hoped that if I took Bernard for a walk this morning, he'd behave this afternoon while I was at art class with Sydney. Our weekly class had been pushed back because of the holidays, and I was dying to see my best friend and catch her up on everything.

It took me a few minutes to figure out how the harness worked—a web of straps with step-in openings for each of his front legs, and a clasp to click together just below the back of his neck. It took me much, much longer to get it on him.

My first thought was to harness him while he was still sleeping. I crept up close, but as soon as I lifted a hoof through the first opening, he squealed and clatter-jumped to his feet. When I approached him, he retreated to a different corner of my bedroom. I made several more attempts. But every time I came within a foot of him, he backed away.

My second thought was, *I need food.*

I closed him in my room so he couldn't escape while I went and retrieved some feed from the bag in the garage. Once I returned, I used a pellet to lure him forward long enough for me to slip the harness beneath his hooves. Unfortunately, it wasn't long enough for me to click together the clasp. He grunted and shuffled away, carrying the harness with him.

Next, I trapped him between the wall and the foot of my bed. I wrapped my arms around his girth and tried to work the harness up and into place. But his short legs and round body made it nearly impossible to see what I was doing. Before I could complete my task, he slipped through my arms to freedom.

Mom took me to a rodeo once. In one of the events, a cowboy riding a horse lassoed a calf, jumped to the ground, and hog-tied the animal by lacing all its feet together and rendering it immobile in a matter of seconds.

I'd never given much thought to the word "hog-tied." I supposed it must've originated with pigs. And even though I hadn't liked watching it be done to the calf, trying to get the pig into a harness made me realize why it might sometimes be necessary.

Luckily, before I grew desperate enough to attempt lassoing the pig from my bed with a jump rope and wrestling him to the ground, Bernard finally gave in to his stomach and allowed himself to be distracted by food again. I dropped a pellet in front of him. As he slurped it up, I seized the opportunity, at last grasping both free ends of the harness and triumphantly clipping them together.

By then, I was almost too tired to go for a walk. And if I'd known how difficult it was going to be, I probably would've given up before we ever started. The pig proved to be impossible on a leash.

I'd gone on many walks with Sydney and her golden retriever, Daisy. Even when Daisy was a puppy, the biggest problem had been getting her to slow down. Until Daisy learned not to tug on the leash, my best friend and I had giggled and run behind her.

Bernard, on the other hand, refused to be hurried. It wasn't that he was incapable of a quickened speed—he'd proved that the day before on the front lawn. No, I was beginning to suspect that Bernard just didn't want to do anything that I desired him to do.

He lazily dawdled behind me down the driveway—stopping four times before we reached the bottom. But I was determined to take my new pet for a walk. I was determined to prove that we could make this arrangement work. I'd toiled so hard to get him into the harness and on a leash. I couldn't give up before we'd even made it to the sidewalk.

When I glanced back toward the house, I saw Emma watching through the front window. From the glint in her eyes, I could tell she enjoyed seeing me struggle.

Even if she didn't care about us all coming together as a family, it was important to me. Mom was happier than she'd been in years and I couldn't risk letting Bernard make things stressful at home. So my determination to tame the wild boar steeled.

Unfortunately, Bernard didn't make it easy. His feet didn't land softly on the concrete sidewalk like Daisy's did. Instead, his comically undersized hooves clanked. And every few feet, Bernard stopped and attempted to bury his snout into the earth. The first time, he got his nose in so deep that he bypassed the blades of grass and unearthed rich chocolate-colored soil before I could stop him. I quickly kicked the dirt back in, hoping Mr. Pine wouldn't notice the new hole in his lawn.

Ten minutes later, we'd only reached the end of the neighbor's property. I could still see the front of Mr. Pine's house. Emma must've had her fill of entertainment, though, because the front window was empty.

Still, I wasn't about to turn back. We sluggishly passed one house after another and finally turned the corner. The retirement community at the end of the block took up as much land as five houses. And apparently, the meticulously kept grounds were even more interesting than all the yards we'd passed. Bernard managed to move impossibly slower. I was starting to worry that we wouldn't make it back home by lunch, and that I'd be late for my art class.

I surveyed the gardens, wondering what could possibly smell so magnificent that Bernard felt the urge to keep his flat snout cemented to the ground. My gaze fell on a familiar face, and we made eye contact before I could pretend that I hadn't seen Liam Rossi.

I glanced around to make sure no one was watching, then reluctantly raised my hand to wave. It's not that I had anything against Liam, really, and I did like his photographs. But if it got back to Sydney that I'd been seen with him, she wouldn't approve.

He had intense eyes, brown with flecks of green. I'd noticed them before. It was like when he looked at something—a person, an object, it didn't matter—he was always thinking something more than he was saying. It was no different now. His smile widened from friendly to amazed when he saw Bernard.

An old man sat on a bench next to where Liam was standing. "Well, gee whiz!" the old man said before whistling appreciatively. "What a fine pig!"

It was nice to know someone thought so. I smiled and let down my guard. Bernard chose that moment to unglue his snout and travel at a pace that nearly dragged me to the ground. Liam and the old man were the first people we'd seen all morning. Most everyone seemed to be huddling indoors on this bright but chilly day after Christmas. Which had been fine by me and Bernard, or so I'd thought. The pig hadn't shown any real interest in people before now. But something about these two was drawing him in faster than I could keep up.

"Whoa, Bernard!" I yelled. "Slow down." The leash pulled tight between us, then suddenly grew slack when the pig halted directly in front of the old man.

"Bernard, huh?" Liam said with a laugh.

The old man wore wire-rimmed glasses. His silver hair was clipped close to his head—where he had hair anyway. He was thin but not frail exactly. "I think someone sniffed out my breakfast," he said, revealing two bite-sized blueberry muffins. "I can share." He leaned forward and let one of the muffins fall to the ground.

Bernard wasted no time inhaling the treat, then smacking his lips together appreciatively. The way he looked at the old man—it was almost like he was smiling.

"Ha!" the man said. "I'd almost forgotten how much vicarious joy can be found in watching a pig eat. Pigs take so much pleasure in consuming food. I am delighted by his delight."

"Um, thank you," I said. I wasn't sure I agreed with his assessment, but he was paying my pig a compliment.

"I'm Francis," the old man said. "If kids today had any social skills whatsoever, George here would've introduced us already. But since he hasn't, what might your name be?"

"I'm Grace," I said. "But who's George?"

Liam hung his head, and a dimple materialized on his left cheek. "You and I both know that an introduction doesn't matter, Francis. You're not going to call her by her real name anyway."

"You're right about that!" Francis said, then turned toward me. "It's a pleasure meeting you, Matilda."

"Matilda?" I asked.

"He does this with everyone," Liam explained. "He says it's 'strategic.' He says if he never calls a person by their right name in the first place, no one will know the difference if he blanks and forgets who they are. So no one will know if his memory is slipping."

"Now don't go giving away all my secrets, Fred," Francis said teasingly. "I've only just met this girl, and I don't want to make a poor impression. She may never bring her pig by again if she thinks I'm a scoundrel."

"No . . . I . . . don't think you're a scoundrel . . ." I said. What I didn't say is that I hadn't yet decided that he wasn't one either.

"Good. 'Cause things don't stick in this old brain"—he tapped the side of his head—"the way they used to."

"Don't believe him." Liam leaned in and whispered. "He's as sharp as anyone I know."

"And my hearing hasn't gone either," he said, shooting Liam a sidelong glance before returning his attention to me. "Now tell me what you're feeding this magnificent beast."

"Uh, pig feed, mostly, but also some table scraps," I added, remembering how Emma had lured Bernard into the house. "Oh, and one upside-down pineapple cake."

Francis puckered his lips together and nodded. "Pigs are smart," he said. "And also motivated by food."

I'd already heard both of these pieces of information from Emma. So far, I'd only seen evidence of the latter.

"That can be a problem," Francis said. "If you're not careful, this pig will end up with spoiled pig syndrome."

"Spoiled pig syndrome?" Was he serious?

Francis nodded solemnly, and I thought that he was. "Yes, don't feed him too many treats, and you've got to let him know who is in charge, or you'll end up with a pig who doesn't respect you. And a disobedient pig is a dangerous pig."

I felt a tingle of apprehension. I might be in over my head, but there was no turning back. With all the drama and upheaval there'd been on Christmas Day, I wasn't about to go home and report that not only was the pig capable of causing a ruckus and ruining dinners, but that he might also become dangerous.

"Not too many treats," I repeated, thinking I wasn't the one who so enjoyed feeding Bernard a blueberry muffin a moment earlier.

"That's right. He'll think of you as nothing but a food dispenser. A belly scratch can be just as good a motivator." To prove his point, Francis reached his liver-spotted wrinkled hand forward and rubbed his fingers back and forth across Bernard's portly underside. The pig flopped to the ground at once, stretching his legs out to the side and closing his eyes as if in a trance.

Liam raised his eyebrows. "Some trick."

While Francis kept scratching, he said, "And don't feel bad

about limiting treats and sticking primarily to feed. Pig pellets don't taste half bad, and I should know."

"You should?" I said, my stomach revolting at the thought.

"Yep, I've sampled my share, along with spoonfuls of dog chow. And let me tell you, the pig feed is far preferable."

"It *is*?"

"Smell, consistency, texture, flavor—in all arenas, pig food is the hands-down winner," Francis said. "Not to mention that it's primarily made of grains with a little molasses to sweeten the pot. Dog food on the other hand, well, there's a great deal of leftover meat parts and by-products that I'd rather not think about."

By then I'd run out of witless replies. I stared at him blankly, still on the fence as to whether he was serious or not. He was a strange old man, which shouldn't have surprised me considering he and Liam seemed thick as thieves. Case in point, Liam had been grinning wildly since the old man started talking about animal feed. "And how do you know all this, Francis?" he asked.

"Well, Chuck, it just so happens that I was a professional pet food taster many years back." He tapped one side of his nose. "Had to put this keen sense of smell, vast animal knowledge, and heightened taste buds to good use somehow. No one wants foul-smelling or tasteless food, not even animals."

"So you ate pet food for a living?" I asked, slightly amazed but mostly disgusted.

"Ah, I never said I *ate* it. I just tasted it. First, I'd rate the odor and then make observations about the food's weight and density. It was very scientific, you know. Then I'd nibble off a little sample, roll it around on my tongue a bit, before spitting it out. After I finished evaluating each sample, I wrote reports and made suggestions. Why, the very food you feed your pig might've been improved because of me," he said proudly.

"Um, thank you?" I said.

Bernard grunted contentedly, still enjoying the belly scratch.

Francis smiled. "This one is a fine animal. He'll make a terrific pet *if* you train him right. You do know how to train him, don't you?" He glanced up, and I swear the old man's eyes bore straight through me.

The anxiety was so intense and sudden, it felt like the pig had been dropped on my chest. I didn't know the first thing about training Bernard. Sure, he looked innocent enough lying there getting his belly scratched. But between the pineapple upside-down cake and the way I couldn't get him to do anything without food, I had some real concerns that he was already on his way to developing spoiled pig syndrome under my care. And a dangerous pig would, no doubt, create more trouble and make Mr. Pine regret his commitment to our family. I needed help.

Francis huffed. "Thought so. Bring him back by here around the same time tomorrow. We'll work on some positive reinforcement."

"Thank you so much!" I said. "That would be great."

"Sweet," Liam said. "I wouldn't dream of missing it."

I stiffened, but there was nothing to be done about it. I couldn't uninvite Liam simply because my best friend would balk at the thought of me hanging out with him. Besides, he was dressed perfectly normal today in a plain gray hoodie, and he hadn't once mentioned bugs. And he seemed to get along well with Bernard. Having him around might not be *that* bad.

Francis stopped scratching Bernard's belly. He sat up straight, a self-satisfied expression on his face. "And bring a fork and baggie of Cheerios."

I'd already stayed longer than I intended and didn't have time to ask why. "Okay, bye," I said, and then hurried out of the garden. I didn't want to be late for art class.

7

Pigs are found on every continent except for Antarctica.

om and I barely spoke on the drive to the art center. She'd mentioned some trouble at work, and I could tell her thoughts were on that. And since I was scarfing down a PB&J on the road because there hadn't been time to eat lunch at home, it's not like I could do much talking anyway. Mom's cell rang just as I was hopping out of the car door. She answered, then blew me a kiss before resuming her phone conversation.

I rushed inside the building, anxious to see Sydney and to vent about my disastrous holiday. Most of the other students had arrived by the time I made it to the art room, but I was bummed to see that my best friend wasn't there yet.

I went straight to the only empty table, and that awkward

feeling that I always have in a room full of kids my age crept in. It went away a few minutes later, when Sydney lowered herself onto the open stool next to mine. Right away, I slid a Polaroid I'd taken of Bernard in front of her. "So much for a dog. *This* was my Christmas present," I said.

"Noooo!" Sydney's eyes went wide. "A pig? It's . . . it's grotesque."

I hadn't expected her to be pleased by the news when I wasn't even pleased myself. But grotesque? I cringed. Granted it wasn't the best photo of Bernard. And he wasn't going to win any beauty contests, but he wasn't grotesque either. In fact, the way the flat disk on his face wriggled around, especially when I came close, was starting to grow on me.

"I'm sorry," she said, and swiftly bit down on one side of her lip. "I mean, a piglet would've been cute. Why not a piglet?"

I shifted my weight, and my stool squeaked on the vinyl floor. The other students turned to look. My cheeks grew warm. When everyone returned their attention to the recycled-paper weaving project we'd started the week before, I answered her in a whisper, "My stepdad said that piglets don't stay small anyway. Most get surrendered when they grow too large."

Sydney's "grotesque" remark had really burrowed under my skin. All day long, I thought I wanted to see my best friend so I could complain to her about the pig, and about Emma. But maybe what I'd really wanted was someone to help me feel better about my situation. Not worse.

"Yeah," Sydney said. "Clearly, that could be a problem. And *you* having a pet pig . . ." She didn't finish her thought.

"What about *me* having a pig?" I bristled.

"Nothing," Sydney said quickly. Too quickly.

"Obviously, you think me having a pig is a bad idea. Why?"

She exhaled loudly, like I was pestering her. "It's just that some people can be really rude and insensitive. That's all." Then she stared me deep in the eyes and added, "I don't want any of our friends to say something mean to you."

That twisted the dagger. I always felt one misstep away from being shunned by our school friends anyway. Did she think Jana and Alejandra would make fun of me? What was she thinking? That they'd compare me to my pig?

Sydney and I had recently clicked through an online article proclaiming it was scientific fact that dogs look like their owners. Sure enough, in all the photos included, the dogs bore a striking resemblance to their humans. We'd chuckled about how much Sydney and her dog, Daisy, looked alike. Is that what Sydney was implying? That Bernard looked like me, after she'd just called him grotesque?

I could feel my face crumble.

"Never mind. You don't need to worry about what anyone

else thinks," Sydney said. "We've been best friends forever. Even if your mom hadn't paid my mom to take care of you, I'm sure we would've been close anyway. That's never going to change."

My mom and her mom met at a prenatal class. We'd played at the park together since we were toddlers. And after my dad left, I started spending even more time with Sydney and her family. First as a favor while Mom completed night classes, then as day care when Mom started working full-time. It sounded like Sydney was saying my mom had paid for her to be my friend. Regardless of her claim otherwise, that didn't seem like a very stable foundation for a friendship. It made me uneasy that she'd brought it up.

"I'm going to go get some more paper," Sydney said with forced cheerfulness. Then she hopped from her stool and visited the supply basket. I sat there stunned until she returned with a handful of paper strips and dumped them on the table in front of us. "There," she said. "Now we have plenty."

I smiled weakly. Maybe I was overreacting. There wasn't any reason to question our friendship. It's just that the thought of us not being best friends was terrifying. I wasn't that close to Jana or Alejandra, or anyone else really. Sure, it would hurt if someone made fun of me because of Bernard, but the scariest thought was going through middle school without Sydney. I couldn't let that happen.

So I let her comments go. I let her take all the purple and blue strips and kept only the brown and gray ones for my project. I listened quietly while she told me about the Christmas presents she'd received—a new flat iron that she gushed about, even though her hair had always been silky and straight anyway. (I didn't want to tell her that I hardly noticed a difference.) A macramé swing chair for the corner of her room that actually did sound amazing. AirPods to go with her new iPhone.

Sydney stopped talking about her gifts long enough to say, "I can't believe your mom still hasn't bought you a phone."

I groaned because what could I say? It's not like I didn't want one.

"Have you even talked to anyone from school over break?" she asked pityingly.

Because I didn't want her to think I was hopelessly pathetic, I blurted out, "Yes."

"Who?" she asked suspiciously.

I paused, torn between telling a lie and prompting more disapproval. "Liam," I said at last.

"Who?"

"Liam Rossi," I said, looking down at my lap.

Sydney grimaced. "Why were you talking to *him*? He's so . . . weird."

"I think he lives in my new neighborhood," I said, forcing

my voice to hold steady. There wasn't any reason I should feel ashamed—it's not like I'd asked to hang out with him. But I also didn't want to sound like I'd enjoyed the time I'd spent with him, even if I had.

"Oh," she said. "I guess that makes sense." Still, I could tell I had dropped down another notch in her eyes.

Sydney's mom picked her up outside the art center after class. She leaned out the open window. "Do you need a ride, Grace?" she asked.

Unlike me and my mom, Sydney and her mom looked a great deal alike. Somehow, they managed to be both elegant and cute, in a Kate Middleton, Duchess of Cambridge, sort of way. Regal, but with dimples.

"No, thank you," I said. "My mom will be here soon."

I watched car after car whiz by on the street in front of the art center. I was bored at first; then I grew concerned. Mom ran a few minutes late now and then when she got tied up at work, or when she couldn't get off an important call. But she'd never been this late before. Worried something awful had happened to her, I started to pace.

I was nearly frantic by the time I recognized a car pulling into the lot. It wasn't Mom's, though. It was Mr. Pine's. And that didn't calm my nerves any.

As soon as his green Subaru hatchback rolled to a stop near

the sidewalk in front of me, I hopped in the back seat and began blasting my stepdad with questions. "Is Mom okay? Why didn't she pick me up? Where is she?"

Mr. Pine swiveled to face me. Unnervingly, he responded as slowly as Bernard had walked to the retirement community. "Everything's fine," he said. "Your mom was called out of town on business."

That must've been the phone call she received when she'd been dropping me off. It'd seemed important, but I'd been too anxious to see Sydney to stick around and find out what it was about.

I didn't like it when Mom traveled for work. I liked it even less when her absence came as a surprise. Grumpy about the entire situation, and about the way Sydney had reacted to Bernard, I could hear the accusation in my words as they came out. "I've been waiting *forever*."

"I was in the middle of shopping when your mom called. What was I supposed to do? Abandon a cart full of groceries in the middle of the store and not have anything to cook for dinner?" Mr. Pine said. He sounded exasperated.

"No," I said quickly, regretting the tone of voice I'd used a second earlier. It already worried me that he thought I was a slob; I didn't want him thinking I was a brat, too. "I'm sorry."

My stepdad turned his face from me, so I couldn't see how

my apology landed. Then he shifted his car into gear and pulled into traffic. The discussion was over.

Angry with myself for slipping up again, and getting short with my stepdad, I turned my head and stared out the window. I stayed that way for the entire ride home. As soon as we got back to Mr. Pine's house, I went straight to the backyard to check on Bernard. He trotted over on his ridiculously under-sized feet with his snout in the air and tail wagging. He seemed excited to see me, which was a nice change. As much as it irked me that he wasn't soft and furry, and that his snout was round and flat instead of heart-shaped, I appreciated his company. With him, I didn't have to worry about being the perfect friend or the perfect stepdaughter. I could just be myself.

I smiled. Something about the way he bounced around on his dainty hooves really was comical. He was comical. *Looking*, that is. My mood soured again, and my smile faltered. Did that mean I was comical-looking, too? I supposed comical-looking was better than grotesque. But I didn't want to be either one.

I rushed inside, leaving the pig in the backyard. Then I raced through the kitchen, down the hallway, and to the bathroom. I studied myself in the mirror. It'd never bothered me before now, but my nose was slightly upturned. I'd always liked my full cheeks—one of the few traits I'd inherited from Mom—but now I wondered if they made my face too round.

"Vain much?" Emma said. She'd been standing in the hall-way watching me and smirking as I'd critiqued my reflection.

My cheeks flushed. I pushed past her, ran down the hallway into my room, and slammed the door behind me. I wanted to cry. This wasn't the first time Mom had traveled since we'd moved in. In fact, she'd gone on two other business trips in the past few months and left me with my stepdad. I'd been nervous about it, but things had gone smoothly. I'd stayed out of his hair and even managed to clean up a few spills without his knowing.

Now that Emma was here, though, it was harder to keep to myself. It was nearly impossible to avoid someone you shared a bathroom with. And between her living right down the hall and me having to rely on Mr. Pine for car rides and meals, I felt out-numbered by strangers in the place I called home.

I need to talk to Sydney, I thought. It was the inclination I always had when something upset me. But as soon as the thought rose in my mind, something twisted in my gut. The notion of talking to my best friend wasn't as comforting as it usually was. Not after our last conversation. So there was nothing to do but hide in my room, feeling more lonesome than ever.

8

Pigs are very smart. Some have outperformed three-year-old human children on cognition tests, and others have been taught to play video games.

Later that evening when I tried to steer Bernard down the hallway and into my room for the night, I was reminded how much I needed Francis's help with training the pig. Bernard blew past my door and pushed Emma's door open with his snout before I could stop him.

"Sorry!" I said, knowing Emma wouldn't appreciate being barged in on. I barely caught a glimpse of her as I corralled the pig with my legs and forced him back the way he had come. She was sitting on her bed, holding a picture frame. Her eyes were puffy and red. Even if she constantly made me feel on edge, I still felt sorry for her. Obviously, she was going through a rough time.

By slipping out of sight before she had a chance to lash out at me, I knew I'd dodged a bullet. I wasn't as lucky with Mr. Pine the following morning. While I was in the kitchen filling a baggie of Cheerios to bring with me to the retirement community, my stepdad slid open the patio door and came charging in from the backyard. Bernard was standing by my feet, no doubt wishing for me to spill the entire contents of the cereal box.

"Your pig is asking for it!" Mr. Pine fumed. Then he disappeared into the garage and returned holding a shovel. The way my stepdad was brandishing the gardening tool, blade side up, as he flew toward us made tiny hairs rise on the back of my neck. Bernard cowered behind my legs, which was about as effective as a toddler attempting to hide behind a flagpole. *What exactly was Bernard asking for?*

The flicker of fear was quickly replaced with curiosity as Mr. Pine stormed past us and back through the sliding patio door. I stepped up to the glass to see where he was headed, and that's when I noticed all the holes in the grass. Apparently while I'd been hiding in my room the evening before, my pig had turned the lawn into Swiss cheese.

Oh no! I thought, and my heart began to race. This was bad.

Clearly agitated, Mr. Pine set to work shoveling freshly excavated earth back into one of the many holes.

I glared at Bernard, but he was oblivious to the trouble he'd caused. He oinked cheerfully and wagged his tail.

I knew I should offer to help, or at the very least apologize—I was responsible for all the damage Bernard had done. But I was supposed to meet Liam and Francis at the retirement community soon. And the thing was, I was too scared to go out there and face my stepfather.

Instead, I wrestled Bernard into his harness, grabbed the baggie of Cheerios and a fork, and fled through the front door. I was more than a little eager to go somewhere where I wouldn't have to worry so much about my behavior, or my pig's. I only hoped Mr. Pine would forgive us.

Walking Bernard wasn't any easier than it had been the day before. I had a death grip on his leash, and my muscles were tight every step of the way. It wasn't until I saw Liam and Francis waiting for us in the garden that some of my tension started to melt away.

"Hi there, Madeline, nice to see you again," Francis said with a wink.

Liam gently nudged him on the shoulder, then said, "Hi, Grace."

I exhaled, expelling a bit more of my anxiety, and then said hello in return.

Even though Bernard had already torn up Mr. Pine's backyard and made a gazillion stops on the way, the first thing he did was ram his snout into the ground and start pushing around the garden soil in a nearby planter bed.

My unease came pouring back in. "Bernard, stop that," I scolded. He ignored me and promptly dug so deep that he unearthed a tulip bulb. I was failing spectacularly at turning him into a well-mannered family pet. If I didn't get things turned around soon, it would only be a matter of time before Mr. Pine grew sick of us. I pleaded with Francis. "I really need your help."

"I'm afraid rooting is a natural instinct for pigs," Francis said. "That's what he's looking for, you know—roots. And insects. Also, pigs are typically iron deficient, but they can get some of the nutrients they need from the soil."

"Insects, like worms?" I asked and then regretted it. I'd never liked worms. Maybe it was better if I didn't know what Bernard was finding buried in the ground.

Liam, on the other hand, perked right up, seemingly excited that the conversation had veered toward one of his favorite topics. "Probably not this time of year," he said. "The worms that don't die off during a freeze go deep when it gets cold."

"Harry here is correct," Francis said. "I believe Bernard would have to dig as much as six feet down to find any worms in the winter." A wistful smile blossomed on the old man's face. "Ah, but that brings back memories."

"What kind of memories?" I asked.

"From when I was a worm picker," Francis said.

"Is that a job?" The thought made my skin crawl but apparently had the opposite effect on Francis. He was glowing with pride.

"Really?" Liam asked skeptically. "I thought you said you were a pet food taster."

"Indeed, I was, and a worm picker before that."

"So you literally picked worms for a living," Liam said. "That's so cool."

I met Liam's eyes, and there was a twinkle of amusement in them that he wouldn't find in mine.

"You'd be surprised how well it pays," Francis said. "If you can handle working from dusk until dawn with a lamp strapped to your head and a coffee can to each leg, well, night crawlers are in high demand."

"A coffee can strapped to each leg?" I asked, trying to picture how strange that would look.

"That's right. One for collecting worms and one for sawdust. A little sawdust on your hands will take the slime away as you pluck the worms from the mud."

"Gross," I said.

"Awesome," Liam said.

"The night crawlers only peak their heads out of the ground when it isn't too hot and it isn't too cold," Francis continued. "As beautiful as this day is for late December, even Bernard isn't going to uncover one. Yet, I imagine he detects the scent of the worms when he sticks his nose in the dirt. Pigs can smell things as deep as twenty-five feet underground. That's why they've been used for centuries to hunt truffles."

"Pigs hunt for chocolates?" I asked.

"Not that kind of truffle," Francis said. "The fancy mushroom kind."

"Oh," I said, feeling embarrassed. I should've known he hadn't meant chocolate. In fact, I had known, sort of, as the comment was coming out of my mouth. But by then, it had been too late to take it back. It was the kind of thing Sydney would make me feel stupid for saying. I snuck a peek at Liam to see if he was laughing at my mistake. He wasn't.

"Were you a truffle hunter, too?" Liam asked.

"Nah, never did hunt for truffles. Someday I'll have to tell you about my other interesting occupations," Francis said with a nod and wink. "But I've eaten my share, and they were worth every penny. Truffles are known as 'the diamonds of the kitchen.' Chefs love to add a shaving or two to a gourmet dish, and they can cost more than a hundred dollars an ounce."

I still wasn't sure what to make of Francis. It wasn't every day that you met someone who'd sampled pet food and expensive delicacies, and who'd picked worms among other "interesting occupations." Half the time I'd been around him, I hadn't known whether to be awed or repulsed.

"They have a particularly pungent aroma and grow as deep as three feet down, usually around the base of an oak or hazelnut tree. The problem with pigs, though, is they'd rather gobble up the tasty gems than turn them over to a human. That's why most truffle hunters today use dogs; they're more easily trained."

I slumped at the reminder that dogs were superior to pigs. My cause was hopeless. I'd never whip Bernard into shape.

"Now wait just a minute!" Francis added, clearly reading my disappointment. "What I *meant* to say is that dogs are more easily trained when it comes to handing over truffles. That's only because food reigns supreme with pigs—you don't ever get between a pig and his meal. More than a few truffle hunters have lost a finger or two in a truffle scuffle with a pig. I've never heard of a single truffle hunter losing a finger to a dog."

I shook my head. If this was supposed to be making me feel better, it wasn't.

"But as I said before," Francis continued, "pigs are very smart. They're highly trainable and are capable of learning things much quicker than dogs."

I glanced at Bernard. His snout was out of the ground now, and he was peering up at me with clear, expressive eyes. It was true—it seemed like there was intelligence behind those eyes, but was there also a twinge of defiance?

"Who do we have here?" An elderly woman scuffled toward us with the aid of a wheeled walker. The walker was hot pink with a zebra-patterned storage pouch hanging off the front. Her ruby-red glasses had wing tips. She stopped short of where we were gathered around Bernard and whistled. "Well, hot hog, I haven't seen a pig in ages," she said.

"You must not be counting the bacon you ate for breakfast," Francis teased. "How are you today, Esmeralda? You're just in time for our training session."

"Don't you listen to him," the woman said. "My name is Alice, and he knows it."

Liam and I introduced ourselves to Alice and welcomed her into our circle. With surprising dexterity, she wheeled her walker around and used it as a seat. "I think this promises to be more entertaining than anything I can find on the tube. I'm sick of soap operas and reality TV."

Francis, who'd been sitting on the same bench as the day before, asked me to hand over the fork and the baggie of Cheerios.

"There you go, always scrounging food off someone," Alice said. "But wouldn't a spoon be more efficient?"

"You've got me on the first count," Francis said. "But the

Cheerios are for the pig and the fork is for his belly. Besides, young Carl here already brought me my daily muffin."

I eyed Liam curiously. If Francis was his grandfather, I didn't see the resemblance. But why else would he be bringing him muffins? Liam smiled back at me and cocked an eyebrow.

Then Francis reached out with the fork in hand and began stroking it along Bernard's belly. The pig immediately flopped to the ground, drawing everyone's interest. Legs outstretched, the pig once again seemed hypnotized by the scratching.

After a few more strokes, Francis said, "You try." In the short moment it took for him to transfer the fork to my hand, Bernard grunted his displeasure at the interruption.

"Keep this up, and in time, he'll associate the fork with a belly scratch," Francis said. "All you'll need to do is pull it out and he'll be putty in your hands. Unfortunately, that may not be enough for him to recognize that you're in charge. You need to make him work for his belly rubs and his food. Reinforce the behaviors you want to see more of. Then, when you tell him to come, or to sit, or stay, he'll do those things automatically."

As I mulled over what Francis was saying, I continued scratching Bernard's underside. The pig grunted again, but this grunt was different from before. It was less of a grunt and more of an oink. And the oinks kept coming in happy little bursts. Despite my skepticism that I could achieve control over the wild animal, I couldn't help but grin at the gleeful noises he was making.

"May I try?" Alice asked.

I passed the fork to her. She was just barely able to reach the pig's belly from her position on the walker. I was glad she could because it seemed to fill her with as much delight as I'd felt. Her eyes glistened behind her ruby-red glasses.

"Okay, now let's make him work for some of that enjoyment," Francis said, clapping his hands and rubbing them together. "Here we go." He opened the bag of Cheerios, and Bernard's snout immediately came to life, wiggling back and forth, sniffing the air.

He jumped to his hooves just as Francis slowly raised one Cheerio above him. "Attaboy," Francis said. "Now sit." He kept the Cheerio just out of reach and slowly backed the pig up. Bernard kept reaching and straining, snout in the air, until his bottom hit the ground. "Good pig. Good, good pig," Francis said, and let the Cheerio fall. Bernard smacked his lips together appreciatively when it landed in his mouth.

"Your turn," Francis said. He was talking to me. "You'll want to use clear words and hand movements whenever you're training him."

I retrieved a Cheerio from the bag. I moved my hand in front of Bernard's snout until his focus was on me. "Sit," I commanded. Then I started to raise the treat above the pig's head, just as I'd watched Francis do. When Bernard lowered his hind end into a seated position, I felt a rush of excitement. "He did it!" I said. "He sat for me!" I felt a swell of hope. Maybe training the pig was possible.

"Magnificent," Francis said. "But don't forget to reward him."

"Oh, right!" I released the treat into Bernard's waiting and surprisingly flexible lips. Lips that seemed able to smile and move around almost as much as his snout. *Dogs don't have lips like that*, I found myself thinking.

"Told you he was smart," Francis said.

Bernard continued to impress as Francis instructed both me and the pig. "Move your fingers back and forth when you want him to follow," he said. "Hold your hand like a stop sign when you want him to stay. Pair a motion with a word every opportunity you get. He'll catch on."

After about ten minutes of training, Francis announced, "That's enough for one day. Don't want to overload him—not with Cheerios or new commands."

"That was the most fun I've had in a decade!" Alice remarked. It seemed like an exaggeration to me, but maybe not by much. "I can't wait to tell my daughter about the pig I met today. I don't know if she'll believe how wonderful he is, though. If only I had a picture to show her when she visits."

"Don't you have a phone to take one?" Liam asked.

I squirmed a little. *Not everyone has a phone.*

"By my nightstand, but no. Not one like you mean. It's a good old-fashioned landline. Hard to take a photo with one of those," Alice joked.

All this talk of things old-fashioned and phones caused a spark in my brain. "I have an idea," I said. "I'll bring my camera tomorrow. I'll take a Polaroid of you with my pig. That is, if you want me to?"

"Hot hog, do I ever!" Alice replied.

Her excitement made me feel like a million bucks. In fact, it was the first time in a long while that I'd felt so at ease. Like I could just be myself instead of being anxious that I'd unsettle Mr. Pine, or that I'd do the wrong thing and displease Sydney.

Spending time in the garden had lifted my worries. But the thought of returning home was still slightly terrifying. I knew Bernard's digging warranted at least an apology, but I was scared to face Mr. Pine, especially with Mom away. I dragged my feet all the way home, expecting a confrontation when I arrived. But it wasn't Mr. Pine waiting to scold me. It was Emma.

9

Pigs have terrible eyesight, but their sense of smell is about 2,000 times greater than that of a human.

Where were you?" Emma said the moment the pig and I stepped through the door.

"I—I—" I stammered, caught off guard by the accusation in her voice. I expected Mr. Pine to be angry, but I couldn't imagine she cared that much about the grass.

Before I could clear my head enough to reply, she snapped, "It really doesn't matter. I don't care where you go, as long as you're not bothering me," Emma said. "What I do care about, though, is when your bad choices affect *my* life. And I'm not exactly thrilled that I'm stuck being your taxi driver, all because you're too self-centered to come home when you're supposed to."

"What?" I had no idea what she was talking about. She'd

never been warm and friendly, but this was the prickliest I'd seen her.

"Dad had an oil change scheduled before Bernard's appointment. But you weren't here, so he had to leave without you. Now *I* have to give you and the pig a ride to the vet," she said crossly.

I'd forgotten about the note. The note I'd found less than a week ago. The note that made me think I was getting an *actual* dog for Christmas. It seemed like decades ago. "Peak Veterinary Clinic?"

"That's the one. And thanks to you, we have nine minutes to drive somewhere fifteen minutes away."

As she hustled me and Bernard back out the door we'd just come through, I wanted to point out that none of this was my fault. Sure, I'd seen the note, but it wasn't like anyone had even told me about it, let alone given me a reminder. If Mom hadn't been called out of town, she would've. But Mr. Pine and his sticky note system left a lot to be desired. Of course, Emma didn't seem like she was in the mood for me to lodge a complaint against her dad. So I kept my mouth shut.

I'd never ridden in Emma's car before. I'd only met her once before she moved in with us two days ago. It registered in my mind that I'd just gotten in a car with a virtual stranger. One with questionable driving skills, I might add. I gripped the handrail on the door. Then I said a silent prayer for my life when she squealed her tires leaving the neighborhood and pushed through a yellow light.

Bernard rode in the back seat, still harnessed and on a leash. His flat disk nose was crinkling like crazy, and he wouldn't stop sniffing in the cracks between the seats. Which came as no surprise considering Emma's car smelled like a combination of air freshener and take-out food.

When Emma slammed on the brakes at a stop sign, Bernard came tumbling forward. He squealed as he rammed into the back of my seat and then slid to the floorboard.

"Bernard!" I gasped as I peered around my headrest to check on him. After finding his eyes were still bright and expressive, and that he seemed unharmed, I whipped my head toward Emma. "Be more careful!" I shouted.

Something like concern flitted across my stepsister's face. Then her gaze hardened, and she said, "What are you so worried about? You don't even like the pig. You'd rather have a dog."

"That's not true," I protested. *Not entirely anyway*, I thought but didn't say.

"Really, then why did you name him Bernard? As in Saint Bernard?"

I clenched my mouth shut and stared out the window,

unhappy that she had caught my drift and now it was coming back to haunt me.

"That's what I thought," she said, like my silence confirmed her suspicions.

She *was* wrong, though. I did like the pig. I especially liked him when we were around Francis and Liam, and Alice, too. But it wasn't that simple. Even though he was growing on me, there was also the twinge of shame I felt when I remembered how Sydney had called him grotesque. Then there was the worry that once winter break was over and the kids at school found out about him, they would make fun of me the way Sydney said they would.

Plus, there was no way around the fact that a dog would've been better for all of us. Bernard had his moments, but he'd caused more trouble than joy so far. And now that I had a pig, it seemed unlikely that Mom and Mr. Pine would allow another pet in the house anytime soon.

Emma and I didn't talk the rest of the way to the veterinary clinic. It was a long twelve minutes. She'd made up time at the beginning, but after that, her driving was noticeably more careful. She didn't, um, make the pig fly again for the remainder of the ride.

Mr. Pine was waiting for us out front. As soon as I'd unloaded Bernard from the back of Emma's car, my stepsister kicked her car into gear and sped away. My stepdad frowned as he watched her go. "I don't imagine she was pleased about having to give you a ride?" He didn't wait for my answer before saying, "Come on, we're three minutes late."

As soon as we passed through the double doors, I wrinkled my nose at the funny, chemical smell, and Bernard snorted. If I found the odor unpleasant, I could only imagine the effect it had on his heightened sense of smell. Thankfully, the clinic wasn't busy. The waiting room was empty, and a lady in scrubs led us right to an examination room. After raising a single eyebrow at Bernard, she let us know that Dr. Chhabra would be with us shortly.

Sure enough, in less than a minute there was a knock on the door, and a compact woman with a warm smile and deep brown eyes let herself in. Dr. Chhabra's movements were slow and measured as she entered. I could tell Bernard liked her at once. His disk nose twitched excitedly when she came near. "Good pig," she said, in a low, calming voice. "Aren't you a handsome fella?" She dropped a treat to the floor for him to gobble up.

I tried to see Bernard through her eyes. I supposed he was handsome—for a pig. His eyes were clear and full of emotion. Rather than resembling a wild hog with beastly tusks, he was tusk-free and had retained some piglet charm even though he was a full-grown mini pig.

"And you must be the lucky owner," she said, turning toward me.

"Lucky, right. That's me," I answered her.

The veterinarian's eyes rested on me a moment longer, and I was certain she had detected the sarcasm in my voice. "I mean, yes, I am lucky," I blurted out, trying to cover for myself.

Mr. Pine, for his part, was oblivious to the exchange. He was held raptured by a cautionary heartworm poster ("Ask your pet's vet about Worm Be Gone NOW!") hanging on the wall.

Dr. Chhabra released me from her scrutinizing stare and began the examination. Bernard let out a few nervous grunts as she looked inside his ears, lifted his tail, then palpated his stomach. "You transported him here in a kennel, correct?"

I swallowed, thinking of how Bernard had flown off the seat at the stop sign. Had he been injured? I shook my head as a powerful wave of anxiety washed over me. "Is he—is he okay?"

She smiled at me warmly. Apparently, the note of concern in my voice had somehow redeemed me for the earlier sarcasm.

"He's more than okay," she said. "He's one of the finest pigs I've met. Not only is he handsome, he's healthy and smart and has a wonderful disposition. But you need to take care of him properly, and that means he should be kenneled when he's riding in a car. And tell me, what are you doing to support his rooting?"

Mr. Pine turned away from the heartworm poster. I tensed.

Now that we were talking about Bernard's digging issues, he'd decided to pay attention.

"It's a natural behavior for him, right? Bernard can't help but dig in the soil, and the dirt gives him iron, too," I said, repeating what I'd learned from Francis. Then I shot Mr. Pine a sidelong glance, hoping he'd be more understanding about the whole thing once he knew why Bernard had done it.

"That's right," Dr. Chhabra said.

"So it's good for him to tear up my lawn?" Mr. Pine's forehead creased, and the words he spoke were followed by a weak groan. Not exactly the reaction I was looking for.

"It doesn't have to be your entire lawn. Set up an area in the backyard for him to root. Bury some treats in the dirt for him, just below the surface. He'll start returning to the same spot. You can do the same thing indoors with a wood box at least two inches high."

I could tell Mr. Pine was listening carefully, but I couldn't gauge the impact Dr. Chhabra's words were having. If it was Mom, I would've known exactly what she was thinking.

Dr. Chhabra continued the exam while peppering in bits of information on diet and best training practices. "Keep in mind," she said, "that no matter how well trained, a pig will always be governed by his stomach. Given the chance, he will get into the trash and open cupboards. He might even find a way to break into the fridge." Some of the information was new, and some—like not giving Bernard too much junk food—I'd already learned at the retirement community.

"Sounds like the diet my wife has me on." Mr. Pine jokingly patted his belly.

But his good mood didn't last long. Once we got back into the car, he inhaled deeply and said, "I think I made a mistake by giving you a pig for Christmas." Then he twisted around in the driver's seat and leaned on the console to get a good look at Bernard. "It's not at all like I thought it would be, and the vet has given me even more to think about. The rescue told me that pigs aren't for everyone. In fact, they guaranteed a three-week trial period. If it doesn't work out, they'll take him back. They'll rehome him elsewhere."

I froze, but my thoughts and emotions were all over the place. On one hand, this felt like an opportunity to get back on track. We could still return Bernard and maybe start all over with a dog. That would be best for the family, wouldn't it? But at the same time, my heart seized in my chest when I thought about never seeing the pig again. Never watching his nose wiggle. Never listening to his blissful oinking as his belly was scratched. Even thinking about sending him back to the rescue felt like such a betrayal.

But the thing that might've concerned me the most was

that Mr. Pine didn't seem to be struggling at all with reversing his decision to bring home a pig. What if Mom and I were on a "trial period," too, and didn't even know it?

It wasn't until Mr. Pine said, "Grace, are you feeling okay?" that I noticed how rigid I'd gone.

"I'm fine," I lied.

"So what do you think?" he pressed.

"I . . . I don't know," I whispered so Bernard wouldn't hear me. Which was silly since he wouldn't understand me anyway.

"To be honest, I can't say I'd be sorry to see him go," Mr. Pine said. "I wouldn't miss his rooting in my grass or having to guard our food all the time so he won't gobble it up. I didn't realize that pigs were so opportunistic."

He probably wouldn't miss the messes I made either, or the outbursts I occasionally still had even though I'd tried so hard to quell them. I couldn't deny how much I longed for a dog, but I didn't want to get rid of Bernard or think that any of us could so easily be disposed of. "Could we, uh, maybe have some more time to decide?" I asked cautiously.

"I don't know, Grace. The longer we keep him, the harder it'll be to part with him. And I'm really having some second thoughts here."

"Please?" I asked as pleasantly as possible. "I'm really sorry about the holes in your lawn. It's only been a few days. We—I mean he," I corrected myself, "he can do better. I know he can."

Mr. Pine considered. "I suppose we can give it a little while longer. We do have almost the full three weeks left in the trial period," he said. Then grumpily added, "I guess that means we need to purchase a kennel."

I felt both sadness and relief. I couldn't believe I might've given up my only shot at getting a dog, but I was thankful I wouldn't have to say goodbye to Bernard. At least, not yet.

We stopped at the nearest pet supply store. It was one of those places where you can bring your pet in on a leash. I wasn't sure I wanted to bring Bernard in, though. I mean, if I had a cute doodle dog, I would've been all over it. But a pig? I was nervous about the looks we'd get. Still, I could hardly leave him in the car. And with Mr. Pine teetering on the edge, I had to do everything I could to convince my stepdad that I was happy with my Christmas present.

Mr. Pine went off to the back of the store to find a large crate—one the pig would fit in and one that would also fit in the back of his hatchback. Meanwhile, I roamed the aisles with Bernard, searching for some of the "intellectually stimulating" toys Dr. Chhabra had mentioned. Bernard's snout was in hyperdrive, crinkling and sniffing the air. His hooves click-clacked on the floor. Sure enough, everyone we encountered stopped what they were doing to gawk at the pig. For his part,

Bernard seemed to be growing accustomed to human attention. Or maybe, like the vet said, he really did have a wonderful disposition for a pig.

Just when I was starting to believe it might be true, he found a display he liked and buried his snout in deep. "No, Bernard!" I scolded, and pulled back on his leash until his face surfaced.

A woman and a small child standing a few feet away stared at us, slack-jawed. "I want a pig, Mommy!" the child cried, with an expression full of awe and wonder. The look on her mom's face, however, bordered on horror.

The woman laughed nervously. "Oh, no, honey. Come on," she said. "Let's go look at the hamsters."

Deciding to remove Bernard from the tantalizing peanut butter-scented treats, I turned a corner and came face-to-face with a friend from school. Technically, Alejandra was more Sydney's friend than mine, but we sat at the same lunch table and shared a few classes. She smiled more than she talked, and she always wore ribbons woven into her long, thick black hair. I froze, waiting for her to notice that the animal at the end of my leash didn't look like any other in the store.

Sure enough, after locking eyes with me, her gaze trailed downward. "Is that *your* pig?" she asked.

"Uh-huh," I said, feeling my cheeks grow warm. I clenched

my eyes shut, waiting for her to start snickering. It was only a matter of time before she drew a comparison between me and my portly pet.

When the silence grew uncomfortable, I peeked out of one eye and then the other.

Alejandra was staring at me. "Are you okay?" she asked.

"Uh-huh," I said again. Bernard took a tentative step forward, his tail wagging side to side. *Swish-swish*, like a windshield wiper, it swept across his rear end.

"Good. Is it all right if I pet him?" Her face broke into a shy grin. "I love pigs."

"Uh-huh," I said, because if something is working for you, why change it?

Bernard's tail wagged some more when she dragged her hand along his back. "He's softer than I thought he would be," she said.

I nodded because I'd noticed the same thing. "Um, he really likes having his belly scratched."

Alejandra moved her hand to Bernard's chest. He snorted dreamily and flopped to one side, right there in the middle of the aisle. Alejandra and I crouched down next to him. She continued to scratch his belly. "I have a cat," she said. "Sometimes, when I scratch her belly, she bites into my wrist and digs her claws into my forearm. Like this." She stopped rubbing Bernard's belly, snatched my arm, and softly poked my skin with her fingernails.

"Ouch!" I cried.

Alejandra pulled back in surprise.

"I mean, you didn't hurt me, but it must hurt when your cat does that," I said, wishing I didn't feel so awkward around people my age. This was why I always let Sydney do the talking.

"Oh, right," she said. "The worst part is, she seems to do it just for fun. She purrs like a demon cat when she attacks. My abuela says she's possessed."

Bernard snorted to let us know he wasn't happy that the belly scratch had been put on pause for our conversation.

Alejandra laughed and began stroking the pig's belly again. "I don't think your pig would ever do anything like that. He's so sweet and adorable," she said.

I smiled. I didn't tell her what Sydney had called him. How could something that was grotesque to one person be adorable to another? Apparently, beauty really was in the eye of the beholder—especially when it came to pigs.

10

**Pigs can get sunburned and will roll in mud
to shield their skin from the sun.**

I t had been important for me to get Bernard under control
from day one, but knowing he was on a trial period made
training him seem increasingly dire. The following morning, I brought out the fork when it was time to slip the harness
on Bernard. I breathed a huge sigh of relief when it worked like
a charm. He immediately flopped to one side and hardly
moved a muscle as I used the fork to scratch his belly with
one hand and worked his legs through the strap openings
with the other. We were a long way from where we needed to
be, but at least the cause wasn't hopeless. And after bumping
into Alejandra at the pet store, I was feeling way more optimis-
tic about my situation.

I was starting to think that there were just as many people

who saw something grand in pigs as there were those who found them repulsive. Once Bernard was properly trained, I knew his good behavior would win more people over—Mr. Pine included.

Bernard and I were off to the retirement community in record time. As we neared the property, I was shocked to see the entire garden area crowded with bodies, canes, walkers, and wheelchairs. When I offered to take a picture of Alice with my pig, I had no idea she'd bring so many friends.

The fifteen or so residents cleared a path for me and Bernard as we made our way to Francis's favorite bench. It's sort of embarrassing to admit, but I occasionally fantasized about being a fashion model and having all eyes on me as I strutted down a catwalk. This was nothing like that.

At first, I wanted to hide beneath a rock. But then, everywhere I looked, the faces were lighting up like flickering candles. And the buzz of excitement got to me. It wasn't so much that I enjoyed all the attention, I just didn't know before then how much I liked making other people feel happy.

Aws of delight rang out as Bernard and I made our way through. And Bernard was really, um, hamming it up, so to speak. He was practically prancing along on his dainty little hooves. A real show pig. "Next time, I'll have to put a top hat and cape on you," I told him. The image I had in my mind made me chuckle. I thought Francis and Liam, and maybe even Mr. Pine, would get a kick out of it, too.

Alice stepped around her flashy pink walker and greeted me with a great big hug. "I hope it's all right that word spread like wildfire," she said. "It's not every day there's an opportunity to have your picture taken with a pig."

Francis was grinning like mad. "This is the best activity turnout we've had in ages," he said.

"No problem," I said. At the same time, I worried I wouldn't have enough film sheets for everyone. Plus, they were all looking to me—literally looking right at me, waiting for instruction, and I had no idea what I was supposed to do. I hadn't planned on running an organized event, certainly not with a crowd this size. And I wasn't sure why I was in charge, other than I was Bernard's owner.

I cast an uneasy glance at the pig. This would never happen if he was a dog. People saw dogs all the time and thought nothing of it. Of course, the pig couldn't help it if he was unusual. And wasn't originality supposed to be a good thing?

I forced a smile, then turned to face the crowd. "Thanks for coming, everyone," I said, projecting my voice as loud as I could. "I guess if you want to, um, form a line or something, I can start taking photos?" It felt weird bossing around people who were more than half a century older than me.

I tried to talk Liam into taking the pictures. He was the one with all the experience. But he gently refused. "No, Grace," he said. "This is your gig."

Those who could walk independently wheeled their friends into place. It was a crooked, bent, and winding line. It was full of kind, expectant eyes and gentle smiles. My heart melted. It was beautiful.

Alice was at the head of the line. Francis surrendered his bench so she could sit down to take a photo next to Bernard. I'd brought along another bag of Cheerios, and I coaxed the pig next to Alice and commanded him to sit. Sure enough, he'd remembered the trick we'd worked on the day before. Francis let out a low whistle, and I beamed. Then we locked gazes and shared a moment of pride. "Good, Bernard!" I said, and let the Cheerio fall into his open mouth. He smacked his lips together and grunted his thanks.

The garden was brown and lifeless in the last days of December. It didn't make for the most desirable background. But in a way, the lack of color only made Bernard stand out more in the pictures. A pink ray of joy surrounded by gray.

Bernard patiently sat through his entire photo shoot as the residents took turns on the bench or with their wheelchairs rolled up beside him. He basked in all the attention and inhaled the doughnut-shaped morsel of cereal I gave him after each photo film popped out of my camera.

Liam disappeared for a few minutes and returned carrying an enormous plastic container of mini muffins. He passed them around, and somehow the food made it all feel more festive, like a party. And Bernard was the star.

As the residents trickled back inside, clutching their Polaroid photos tight, Liam, Francis, and I drifted back to our bench. "That was some gathering!" Francis said.

"A pig does make an interesting party guest," Liam added, glancing down at Bernard. By then, Bernard had fallen fast asleep, tuckered out by all the excitement.

"Agreed," said Francis. "Almost as thrilling as a manatee." Francis had his eyebrows raised, and I could tell he was trying to pique our curiosity again.

I decided to play along. "Are you saying you've been to a party with a manatee?"

"That's right. An underwater pizza party, in fact."

Liam caught my eye, and his face broke into a grin. "So in addition to being a pet food taster and a worm picker, what were you?" Liam asked. "Like a trainer at an aquarium or something?"

"Oh, no, nothing like that. Although I did attempt to train fleas for a circus when I was younger, but that was just a hobby, and another story. No, I was a scuba-diver pizza delivery man for an underwater hotel in Key Largo. Now, one time, when I arrived at the air lock with three large pizzas in my waterproof case, I was invited to stay. It was a costumed birthday party for eight-year-old triplets. Let's see, the parents were both dressed as crabs, one child was an octopus, another a shark, and the third was a sea turtle. In my dive gear, I completed the entourage."

"What about the manatee?" Liam asked.

"I'm getting there," Francis said. "The children devoured the pizza and were just about to cut into the cake, when an enormous manatee swam up to the domed glass window. He peered in, and I swear, he was as interested in us as we were in him. His hefty jowls bubbled, his tail swayed, and he folded his flippers across his belly and rolled. If I didn't know better, I would've sworn he was laughing at us in our costumes. Like Bernard was today, he was the highlight of the evening."

I'd always wanted to see a manatee. There was something sweet and endearing about their tubby bodies, soulful eyes, and broad noses. I knew they were called sea cows, but now I wondered if "sea pig" might be just as fitting. Francis's story also jiggled something loose in my brain, and I remembered the thought I'd had walking through all the residents. "I want to get Bernard a costume," I said.

"What kind?" Liam asked.

"I don't know . . . I was thinking maybe a top hat and a cape." I worried my bottom lip. Now that I'd said it aloud, the idea seemed silly.

"That would be amazing," Liam said.

"You think so?" I asked. "The vet said pigs can get sunburned. So I thought maybe a cape would help protect his skin in the summer."

Liam nodded his head enthusiastically while I glanced at my toes. I hadn't really thought about my future as a pig owner before then. Summer seemed so far away, so far beyond the three-week trial period. I could see it, though—me happily walking the pig to the retirement community when the sky was bright and the world was green again. I liked the idea so much that it hurt to think it might not happen.

"Huh, I've seen a great many things," Francis said, "but I can honestly say I've never seen a live pig in a top hat and cape. There are few things left in this life that would thrill me more. I tell you, that's the picture I want to take with this delightful pig—one where he's dressed in his finest attire."

Francis was right. Bernard was delightful. Seeing him interact with everyone at the retirement community, seeing how elated they were to pet him, to pose for a photo with him—it all made me see Bernard in a new light. If only I could get Mr. Pine to see it, too.

In all the chaos, I hadn't gotten around to taking a Polaroid of Francis with Bernard. "How about I promise to take a picture like that if you promise to keep helping me train him," I said, even though I had no idea where I'd come up with a pig costume.

"Deal," Francis said, and we shook on it. "But I think Bernard has had enough excitement for today." As if to punctuate his point, the pig let out a loud snore, and we all laughed. "We'll have to continue his training tomorrow."

I had to gently nudge the pig awake, and then Liam left the retirement community at the same time as us. He fell into step beside me. I felt an initial rush of unease. As rocky as things were with Sydney right now, I couldn't afford to be seen with him. And yet . . . I liked being around him. He made me feel comfortable being me. "It was nice of you to bring those," I said, gesturing at the emptied plastic container he carried with him.

"My dad drives a delivery truck for a bread company. He brings home extras with him all the time. Everyone else in my family is tired of eating mini blueberry muffins. But I don't ever get sick of them," he said, then added, "The muffins, not my family."

"So you do get sick of your family, then?" I asked teasingly.

He grinned and rubbed the back of his neck with one hand. His cheeks turned a pleasant shade of pink. "Well, I guess you could say that. I'm the oldest of seven, so it gets kinda loud at my house sometimes."

"Seven?" I said. "Wow." I'd been going to school with Liam for years, and I never knew he came from such a large family. I guess I didn't know much about him at all. I also couldn't imagine how there was ever any peace in a family that size. But the twinkle in Liam's eye told me that they were happy.

"Yeah, I have four sisters and two brothers," he said. "You? Do you have any siblings?" The way he deflected the attention made me think that, unlike Francis, he didn't like talking about himself.

"No, I'm an only child," I said. Then I remembered Emma. "I mean, sort of. I have an older stepsister?" It wasn't supposed to come out sounding like a question. But I guess my relationship with her and Mr. Pine was, well, questionable. *Trial period*, said an ugly little voice in the back of my head.

I felt Liam's intense hazel eyes on me as I looked straight ahead and quieted the voice. It crossed my mind that a boy was walking me home, and this felt significant—like something I might want to share with my best friend. Only, I knew all too well how Sydney would respond, considering the identity of said boy.

"Do you get along with her?" Liam asked after a spell.

Even though I wasn't looking at him, I could tell he was

smiling. When I peered out of the corner of my eye, he was rubbing the back of his neck again. I thought it might be something he did when he was nervous. I also thought it was kind of cute the way his hair fell forward and his head hung sort of shyly when he did it. *He* might be cute.

"No," I said, forcefully dragging my thoughts away from the dimple in his cheek and back to answering his question. "I don't. Everything about me seems to annoy her."

Liam laughed, and I felt a stab of hurt, thinking he might agree with Emma that I was annoying. Also, that maybe his dimple wasn't so adorable after all.

Then he said, "My mom says that's what younger siblings are for. Why do you think I've been spending hours at a retirement community over winter break?"

"To get away from your noisy brothers and sisters—I didn't know," I said honestly. I'd walked by the retirement community at least a dozen times before Bernard came into my life. I hadn't once considered stopping before Liam and Francis waved me over.

"I thought maybe you were visiting a relative," I added. Francis and Liam didn't look anything alike, but it was still possible that they were family.

"Nah, I just met Francis at the start of break. I kept seeing him outside my window—my yard backs up to the retirement community grounds. To be honest, he seemed kind of depressed, sitting all alone on his bench."

"Francis? It's hard to imagine him ever being sad."

"I know, right? But he did, and one day my baby sister was crying, and my brothers were wrestling over an Xbox controller, and my mom was yelling at my brothers to stop fighting, and I was wishing I could make them all disappear when Francis and I locked eyes through the window. He tipped his head at me and flashed me a knowing smile. It was like this . . . this understanding passed between us. Like we were both stuck places we'd rather not be. The next day, I hopped my fence and brought him a mini blueberry muffin."

"Do you really wish your family would disappear?" I asked. The thought was unsettling. Was that the way things were when younger siblings came into the picture? Was there no hope for Emma ever accepting me?

"Nah, of course not," Liam said. "Just in that moment, you know." Liam grinned, and that was that. It was final—he and his dimple were decidedly cute.

"Yeah." I answered like it was the same for me, but it wasn't. There were no doubts in my mind that Emma wanted me to disappear in *all* the moments. Either way, I was glad Liam had decided to start visiting Francis. I was even gladder that I'd stopped to talk to them both that day. It also occurred to me that Liam was walking with me and Bernard, not because we happened to be going the same direction—his home was near the retirement community—but because he wanted to. Did that mean he liked me?

"Bernard was a hit today," Liam said, changing the subject. "He'd make a good therapy pig."

"A therapy pig?" I said. "I've heard of therapy dogs but not therapy pigs."

"Dogs, birds, llamas, reptiles, cats—why not pigs, too? You saw how excited everyone was to spend time with Bernard. Of course, pigs are good therapy."

"I guess," I said. It wasn't something I'd really considered, but maybe I should. I didn't know much about therapy animals. What I did know was that they visited people at places like hospitals, libraries, schools, and nursing homes. And they provided comfort and affection to people who needed it the most.

Then it hit me. People who volunteered their time and shared their animals in this way were generous and kind. No one would ever think of them as difficult or self-centered. If Bernard became a therapy pig and me his handler, Mr. Pine couldn't help but be proud of us both, and Emma would have to see that I was giving and selfless, not spoiled and vain. And Bernard and I would be a team, doing good and spreading joy in the world. Mr. Pine wouldn't dream of breaking that up by rehoming my pig. I felt a rush of energy and determination.

I sprang at Liam and wrapped my arms around him snugly, surprising us both. I'd gone from being worried about being seen with him to hugging him tight in a matter of minutes. That wasn't good. My actions needed to be more predictable, more controlled than that. Remembering myself, I pulled back quickly before he had time to hide the happily bewildered expression on his face. He looked like, well, like a child on Christmas morning—one who *had* received a puppy.

"Er, sorry," I said, before blurting out, "Thanks!" Then Bernard and I continued on our way, leaving poor Liam standing dumbstruck as he watched us go.

11

Pigs are not dirty! They're actually very clean animals, but they will roll in the mud to cool off. They must since they have very few sweat glands.

The first thing I did when I got home was jump online to research therapy pigs. It was bad enough that Mom was gone, but she'd also taken her laptop with her. That meant I had to use the desktop computer my stepdad moved to the basement along with all his office furniture.

I'd been given permission, but it still felt weird using Mr. Pine's computer. Not only that, it was a bit like a dungeon downstairs. Mom had placed a colorful area rug beneath the desk, but the unfinished basement was chilly with its concrete walls and concrete floors. If I were Mr. Pine, I'd be itching to move back upstairs, but that would mean someone would have to go. I tried not to think about that as I dove headfirst into my research.

Liam had been right that pigs could be trained and certified as therapy animals. I scanned through the requirements. There was a long list of skills Bernard would have to learn. They seemed overwhelming but doable considering how fast Francis had taught Bernard how to sit on command. I felt a swell of pride thinking how grateful I was that pigs learned faster than dogs. Then my eyes landed on something that drained my optimism in a heartbeat: "The certification process takes a minimum of six months to complete."

Six months? The trial period would be up in a little over two weeks. It felt like such a blow, but not all hope was lost. Maybe if Bernard and I weren't certified yet, but we were enrolled in a program, Mr. Pine would be less likely to break apart our team.

I read on: "Handlers can be as young as ten. However, an adult co-handler is required to complete the program as well as accompany the animal and minor on all visits."

Blow number two. Mom was obviously my first (only?) choice, but as busy as she was with her new promotion, I didn't know if she'd have time. Also, with Mr. Pine leaning toward rehoming Bernard, the clock was ticking and I'd have to wait two more days until she came home to even ask her.

I was feeling deflated enough, but then at dinner, Emma let loose. There's this word—"lambasted"—that my mom uses to describe when one company head verbally attacks another while she's mediating a merger meeting. Well, Emma, *lambasted* me.

It started with a complaint about a smudge of toothpaste I'd left in the bathroom sink. Then, apparently, she'd been "disgusted" to find a lock of my hair in the shower drain. Next thing I knew, Mr. Pine was glowering as Emma criticized everything from my choice in music (I had no idea she could hear it playing from her bedroom) to my new(ish) tennis shoes that were apparently more expensive than any shoes her dad ever bought for her, to the amount of time I'd spent watching Netflix that afternoon, even though it was winter break and Bernard had been sleeping, and with Mom gone, there'd been nothing else to do.

Everything she was complaining about had obviously bothered him, too. But some sort of parental code kept him from joining in on the vitriol. "Now, Emma—" Mr. Pine feebly started to placate her, but she talked right over him. So he merely shoved another bite of couscous into his mouth.

"And I can't find my diamond stud. I left it on the bathroom shelf, and now it's gone. The hole in my nose is going to close if I don't put it back in soon. I know *she* took it," Emma said, pointing a finger accusingly at me.

I sat motionless in my chair, feeling humiliated, but also angry and defensive. First of all, I did no such thing. I would never touch *anything* that came from Emma's nose. Still, I had to admit that I'd sensed her resentment building the past few days. The energy she gave off when we passed each other in the hallway or found ourselves in the same room had been seething. But this was the first time she'd openly expressed her animosity toward me.

As soon as the stun wore off, my fear of Mr. Pine's reaction kept me from returning fire. I wanted to blast back with all my might that she wasn't perfect either. She left her makeup splayed over the bathroom counter, I didn't care for her taste in music either, and she was a horrible driver! If my stepdad decided the hostility and conflict wasn't worth it, though, and that one of us would have to go, I knew which one he'd choose.

It just about killed me to remain silent, but I did. The damage had already been done. Retaliation would only make things worse. I peered at Mr. Pine out of the corner of my eye, expecting to find disapproval and scorn.

Instead, I found him choking on his food, spewing tiny balls of grain all over the kitchen table before covering up a grim smile with his napkin. That was the thing about Mr. Pine—I never knew what to expect. He may have agreed with Emma on all other counts, but at least he didn't seem upset that the diamond stud had gone missing.

More worrisome than anything else that had transpired over the course of dinner, though, was the way a light bulb seemed to suddenly go on above his head. He set his napkin down and didn't even try to hide the expression of satisfaction blooming on his face. "Emma," he said, "what could Grace possibly want with your nose stud? I'm sure it will turn up, and if it doesn't, well . . ." He didn't finish that thought, before adding, "I'm going to go call Grace's mother now. Excuse me." Then he abruptly stood up from the table.

As soon as he'd left the kitchen, Emma said, "What was that about?"

Mr. Pine's sudden departure left me feeling more unsettled than confused. But I wasn't about to share my apprehension with my stepsister. Certainly not after the way she'd just treated me. So I shrugged my shoulders as I shoveled a bite of couscous into my own mouth.

Even if it was a long shot, having a goal helped me take my mind off my troubles at home. I didn't let Francis or Liam know how badly I wanted to get Bernard certified as a therapy pig, though. I didn't mention it at all, because it still felt too much like a wish. If I said something about it to anyone, it might not come true. But I made sure we worked on the skills necessary to complete the program. With Francis's help, Bernard had mastered "sit" and was doing very well on "come" and "stay." I knew the biggest challenge would be teaching Bernard to "leave it," when he was so keen on vacuuming up everything in sight.

While we made the pig perform for his Cheerios, Liam elicited stories from Francis. And Francis, for his part, seemed more than happy to oblige.

"Have you had any other interesting jobs?" Liam asked.

"Why, yes, as a matter of fact," Francis said. "Once I decided worms were too small and slimy, I moved on to snakes."

"You picked snakes?" I asked, imagining coffee cans full of writhing snakes strapped to a young Francis's legs as he plucked them from fields of wild grasses. It seemed a bit of a stretch. Unlike worms, I thought the snakes would slither right out of the can.

"Not picked," Francis corrected. "Milked."

"You milked snakes?" I asked. Now I really didn't believe him. Even Bernard seemed to detect a lie. He snuffled his snout in the air like he smelled something putrid.

"Um, I'm pretty sure snakes don't have udders," Liam pointed out, which made me chuckle. He and I made eye contact, but I couldn't hold it. I felt a zip of heat before I darted my gaze elsewhere.

"Laugh all you want, but it's an extremely dangerous job," Francis said. "Fatal even, if you don't handle the snakes properly. You're right that they don't have udders, but some snakes do have sacs of venom—in their heads usually right behind their eyes." Francis drew one of his crooked fingers to his temple.

"And that venom is extremely valuable. It's needed to make antivenom—which is the only treatment for certain venomous snake bites. Plus, it can be used to treat a number of other afflictions, *if* you can safely extract it."

Liam's right eyebrow quirked slightly. "And how do you do that?"

"Very carefully," Francis said, meeting Liam's stare. "First you use a long pole with a curved end to hook the snake. Then you pin its head between your fingers like this." Francis held his hand toward us, making it into the shape of a clamp. "You have to get the snake to bite down on the edge of a glass vial." He made a swift clawing motion at the air. "And force it to penetrate a thin rubber cap with its fangs. That causes the same effect as if it were biting into prey, which in turn stimulates the release of venom into the vial for collection."

I grimaced. Snake milking sounded even worse that worm picking. "Can we talk about something else?" I groaned.

"What would you like to talk about?" Francis asked.

Bernard grunted just then. Apparently, he wanted to alert us to the fact that we'd stopped feeding him Cheerios and weren't paying him nearly enough attention. I drew out the fork I'd been carrying in my back pocket, and he instantly collapsed to the ground. I settled down on the cold grass beside him and began scratching.

"How about pigs?" Liam asked. "What else do you know about them?"

"Hmm, let's see . . . For starters, have you heard the expression 'sweating like a pig'?"

Liam nodded.

"It doesn't mean what you think. Pigs don't sweat. They can't. They don't have hardly any sweat glands. That's why they roll in the mud—to cool themselves off. The expression came from a type of iron called 'pig iron,' because after being smelted, the pieces resembled a sow and piglets. And as the iron cooled, beads of moisture would form on its surface.

"Also, if anyone ever calls you a 'dirty pig,' or says your room is a 'pigsty,' meaning it's messy, they don't know much about pigs. Pigs are naturally clean animals."

As I listened to Francis talk, I wondered how many more things people got wrong, not just about pigs, but about one another. Emma was wrong about me. I wasn't spoiled, and I wasn't a pest. And as I watched Liam and how he engaged Francis, I thought how Sydney was wrong about him. He wasn't weird. He was curious, smart, and kind. Of course, while I was thinking this, he was steering the conversation away from pig misconceptions, to Dáin Ironfoot, a pig-riding dwarf in *The Hobbit* movie.

Francis said, "You know, it's not all that far-fetched. Pigs were used to combat war elephants in ancient Rome. Their loud squeals frightened away the giant beasts."

Liam's face lit up. "That's sick," he said, and I thought, *Okay, maybe he is a little weird, but in a good way.*

. . .

Mom finally came home on the last day of winter break. By then, not only could Bernard sit, stay, and come on command, he also knew how to twirl, shake, and honk a horn that belonged to one of Liam's sisters. Bernard was a fast learner, and we'd practiced most of the skills required for him to become a therapy pig. The only one Francis and I hadn't covered yet was "leave it." I was saving it for last because I knew it would be the most challenging one for Bernard to master. Still, I believed with all my heart that he would make a terrific therapy pig, and that the hardest part would be convincing Mom.

She was exhausted from traveling, but she wanted to have a special night, just me and her. Well, me, her, and Bernard, that is. Mr. Pine took Emma out to dinner. Mom and I stayed home, popped popcorn, and put in a movie like we used to do.

After Bernard performed all his new tricks for Mom, he crashed in a pile of blankets at the foot of the couch.

"He's quite the entertainer," Mom said.

"I know . . ." I said, thinking this was my opening. "About

that, I want to get him certified to be a therapy animal. I'd like to get him a costume—a cape and a top hat—and visit people to cheer them up."

"I see." Mom cast me a wan smile. The way she paused for a nanosecond was maddening. Judging by the look on her face, I knew I wouldn't like what came next, and I was right. "But, honey, you've only had him for a short time," she said. "Don't you think you might be rushing things? Having a pet is a big responsibility. I don't know that you need to jump right into a certification program and community service, too." She breathed in and out through her nose in a decidedly uneasy manner, then added, "And, well, we're still not sure that the pig is going to work out."

I knew then that she and Mr. Pine had been discussing the trial period. My stomach roiled, and I felt a rush of heat rise in the tips of my ears. I was angry and nauseous and disheartened all at once. Mom and I had been a team before Mr. Pine came into the picture. This felt like she was changing sides. And I remembered how I thought a dog would balance things out.

Then, as if Mom was reading my mind, she said, "It might be best if the pig is rehomed. Maybe we can investigate adopting a puppy this summer instead. Nathan thought he was doing the right thing, but his timing was awful, and his decision was too impulsive."

"His name is Bernard," I said, choking up. "He's not 'the pig' or 'a pig'—he's Bernard. And . . . and . . . you can't make me give him up. You just can't."

"Oh, Grace," Mom said, pinching a strand of my hair and tucking it behind my ear. "I know it won't be easy. But please give it some thought. We all misstep in life. And sometimes it takes a little going backward before you can go forward to find the right path again. Do you understand what I'm saying?"

I shook my head.

"The pig—"

I glared at her, and she corrected herself. "I *mean* Bernard. Bernard was a mistake. A well-intentioned mistake but a mistake nonetheless. I'm so sorry. The last thing your stepdad and I want is to see you get hurt. But we think it might be better for our family in the long run if we return the—er, Bernard. I know he was your Christmas present . . . maybe it's time to get you the phone you've been wanting instead."

I couldn't believe my ears. Returning Bernard would not be "better for our family." And Mom was resorting to bribery. "Mom, he's different!" I protested. "He's not the same pig who ruined our Christmas dinner. I've been training him. And . . . and bringing him to the retirement community—they love him there! You and Mr. Pine will love him, too, if you just give him a chance."

I sat up straight and tucked my legs beneath me on the couch. "Please," I begged.

Mom tipped her head and stared at the ceiling. It was what she did when she was working out a problem. Then she briefly closed her eyes before dropping her chin and meeting my gaze. "I thought you were going to be more receptive to the idea of rehoming Bernard. I guess we still have some time . . ."

I didn't have even a moment of relief that the decision was being put off before Mom dropped another bombshell. "But we'll need to get this sorted out next week . . . when I get back."

"What do you mean?" I gawked at her. "You *are* back."

It felt like eons since we'd actually been watching the movie, but Mom put it on pause anyway. She repositioned herself on the couch so that her entire body was turned toward me. "Grace," she said, and sighed. "I know you're not going to like this either, but your stepdad and I are . . . well . . . we're taking a vacation."

"When?" Admittedly a vacation was better than a rift in the family, but it still made me feel incredibly anxious.

"Tomorrow."

"You're kidding, right? You just got home." I threw up my hands and accidentally bumped the popcorn bowl, sending a handful of puffs onto the floor. Even though he had been sound asleep, Bernard's snout wiggled and sniffed. Next thing

I knew, he was there to vacuum up the mess. "Leave it," I said. Granted, it came out weak considering the circumstances, but I was still disheartened to a greater degree when Bernard chose to ignore me in favor of the buttery popped kernels.

Mom sighed again. "I know. Traveling so soon after a business trip isn't ideal. But I have some time off now. And Nathan and I weren't ever able to go on a honeymoon. It seemed like too much to ask of Sydney's family, and we didn't have anyone to stay with you. But now we do." She held my gaze again, no doubt watching for my reaction.

"Nooooo," I said. "Who? Emma. No, no, no." I knew they'd never leave me by myself, but what Mom didn't realize was that leaving me with my stepsister would be so much worse. Mr. Pine knew how much she loathed me, but that obviously didn't matter to him. He needed a break from all the disorder my pig and I were causing, and now he was going to get one. I only hoped it wouldn't turn into something more extended. "This was Mr. Pine's idea, wasn't it?"

"I really wish you'd stop calling him that," Mom deflected. "Look, I know you're not comfortable with calling him 'Dad,' but 'Mr. Pine' is so formal. Couldn't you try 'Nathan' or 'Nate'?"

I ignored her and narrowed my eyes. "This is why he called you the other night, isn't it?"

"Yes," Mom conceded. "We're concerned with how things

are going. You and Emma will be living together for the fore-seeable future. Without me and Nathan here to intervene while we're on vacation, it'll force the two of you to rely on each other—to develop some trust."

"Mom, this isn't one of your team-building activities," I said. "Emma and I are not employees from separate businesses who need to learn how to work together. She hates me."

"She doesn't hate you." Mom tucked another loose strand of my hair behind my ear. "I don't see how anyone could hate you."

"She—" I didn't know how to put into words that Emma would never accept me. Not only that, I feared she would do everything within her power to rip this family apart. She had nothing to lose and everything to gain by pushing me and Mom out of her and her dad's life. But before I could explain all that, the front door flew open and Emma stormed into the house with Mr. Pine on her heels. "Emma, wait!" he said.

My stepsister paused only long enough to cast me a murderous glare. Then she stomped down the hallway and slammed her bedroom door shut. Clearly, she'd heard the news, too.

"Mom," I said. "She *hates* me."

12

An average litter size is ten piglets. The largest litter ever recorded included thirty-seven piglets in 1993.

The moment our parents dragged their suitcases out the front door bright and early the next day, there was zero percent relying on each other, and one hundred percent contempt between me and Emma. She spoke to Bernard. I spoke to Bernard. But neither of us spoke to the other.

Breakfast went something like this:

Emma: I think someone left nothing but crumbs in the cereal box. But you would never do something so inconsiderate, would you, Bernard? You're a good pig.

Bernard: *snout wiggles*

Me: I think someone forgot to shower this morning. But it wasn't you, Bernard. You smell like maple syrup.

Bernard: *wagging tail and happy grunts*

Like so, my stepsister and I managed to carry on with our morning routine, without ever truly acknowledging each other's existence.

Before she left, Mom had made a suggestion. "Now that Emma is living with us, she might be able to give you a ride on her way to the high school. I know how much you dislike riding the bus." Apparently, she didn't understand how much *more* I disliked riding with Emma. Also, the bus was a far safer option.

Before grabbing my backpack and heading out the door, I put Bernard in the garage for the day. The outside world had been coated with a fresh layer of frost. We'd had unseasonably warm weather the week after Christmas. But now, like winter break, it was over. At least the garage had been nice and toasty since Mr. Pine added an overhead heater.

Bernard looked up at me eagerly, and I could tell exactly what he was thinking. Not only would he not fight me when I tried to harness him, he would welcome it. "No walk to see Francis and Liam today," I said sadly. "It's too cold, and I have to go to school." I wondered if Francis would miss us as much as I'd miss visiting him. *Maybe more,* I thought. Unlike Mom, he loved Bernard and had plenty of time on his hands.

He loved Bernard and had plenty of time on his hands! I don't know why it hadn't occurred to me sooner, but Francis would be the perfect co-handler. Mom wasn't my only option. With her schedule and reservations about Bernard, I'd started to think my plan was doomed. Maybe it wasn't, though. Francis already knew so much about training pigs, and all the certification program said was that one of the handlers had to be an adult. It didn't say anything about the adult being my legal guardian.

Bernard rubbed against my pant leg just then. I leaned over, threw my arms around him, and planted a kiss right on his forehead. "Maybe there's hope for us after all! Please be good while I'm at school," I pleaded. Despite Mom's objections, I was more determined than ever to turn Bernard into a well-mannered therapy pig. I wanted to march to the retirement community right that minute and ask Francis to take the certification classes with me. But ditching school would not help my cause any. Last thing I needed was for Mr. Pine to think I had a truancy problem along with everything else. It would have to wait.

"Okay," I said to Bernard. "Here's the plan. I don't know how, but I'm going to talk to Francis about the therapy animal program *and* get you a costume before Mom and Mr. Pine get back from their trip. Not just any costume. It has to melt their hearts so they can see you the way I see you. If we can show Mom and Mr. Pine just how wonderful you are, I know you'll sail right through the trial period. You'll be mine forever."

Bernard oinked cheerfully, and I planted a second kiss upon his wrinkly forehead.

It was extra chilly waiting at the bus stop. My breath formed little white clouds in the air. It was hard enough going back to school. I didn't like leaving Bernard, and I didn't like that the issue of his trial period was unresolved. The freezing morning made it even more miserable. At least the bus driver had the heat on full blast. I climbed aboard, and more than the higher temperature inside, the sight of a familiar face warmed me.

Liam sat up straighter in his seat as I entered the aisle. How was it that I'd never dreamed of sitting next to him in the months previous to break that we'd ridden the bus together?

Now, considering all the days we'd spent together at the retirement community, I couldn't possibly sit next to my usual seatmate, Jana. Most of our rides to school had consisted of her telling me about where she'd traveled for her latest dance competition, what type of routine she performed, or, on the rare occasion that she hadn't just won some dance award or scholarship for her ultra-expensive lessons, she'd talk about the hottest viral meme, making me feel even more out of touch since I didn't have a phone and, therefore, was in the dark on most things social media related.

I knew she'd have an earful to give about her trip to New York, and I couldn't stomach that today. So I smiled and waved as I passed her by and opted for the open seat next to Liam.

"Hi," he said, his hazel eyes shining.

"Hi," I said. Sydney would freak when she heard about this. But I needed to feel something warm and caring after Emma's hostility. And how had I not noticed before that Liam practically radiated kindness?

It was awkward for about two seconds. Then we started talking about Bernard and how his training was going, and Francis and his stories. Then I asked Liam about photography club and if he'd used his camera much over break. He told me he'd taken portraits of each of his family members and presented them as Christmas gifts. As he talked about trying to tell a story with each of his photos—capturing the essence of his mom's strength and his little brother's indomitable spirit—it made me want to practice my skills. The residents of the retirement community had seemed so appreciative of my Polaroids, but I knew I could do better.

It all felt so familiar and comfortable. Far more comfortable than if I'd sat next to Jana. It's not that I had anything against dance. It's just that it got tiresome listening to her talk about herself all the time.

This was the closest I'd been to Liam since I'd lunged at him with a hug. Our bodies were crammed together on the small seat. We'd only ever been around each other outdoors up until now. I could smell his boy smell and a touch of sweetness on him. Maybe a slight hint of blueberry crumble? And it made me smile to think of him gobbling up the mini muffins the rest of his large family rejected. I glanced down and noticed the backpack by his feet. It looked brand-new and it was mustard-colored with colorful beetles printed all over it.

"You really like insects, don't you?" I asked, gesturing toward his backpack.

"It was a Christmas present from my younger siblings, but yeah, we all do," he said shyly.

The thought of him and his brothers and sisters bonding over bugs was sweet, but I worried everyone at school might not see it that way. I changed the subject. "I wish we could visit the retirement center today," I said. I didn't mention that I had an important question to ask Francis.

"Me too. If only we didn't have to be at school during the middle of the day when it's the warmest," he grumbled. "It'll be too cold after school, and after my homework is done. Francis doesn't complain too much, but I think he gets chilled sometimes out in the garden even when the sun is out."

I shifted uncomfortably in my seat. I wanted to recruit Francis as soon as possible, but Liam was right. It probably would be too cold to visit later in the day. The same would be true for the rest of the week.

"I told him I'd come by to visit on Saturday, though." He paused, and I felt his gaze dart to me; then it quickly bounced back to the seat in front of us. "What about you?"

"I wouldn't miss it for the world," I said.

I heard him release his breath. He turned his head away so that he was staring out the window. But before he did, I caught a flash of the pink coloring his cheeks, and it reddened mine, too.

Even though I was grieving the end of winter break and not being able to visit Francis, my morning classes weren't that bad. The boost sitting next to Liam on the bus gave me, combined with the more hopeful outlook I had for me and Bernard, made social studies and pre-algebra far more tolerable.

On the way to the cafeteria for lunch, Sydney snuck up on me and looped her arm through mine. "Hey there, stranger," she cooed in my ear.

"Hey," I answered, and felt a jolt of something course through me. That was the thing about Sydney. She was electrifying. She was a field of energy, and as long as you were welcomed inside it, you felt protected. You felt lifted above ridicule and embarrassment—almost untouchable. But a twinge of worry underscored the sudden confidence boost. Sooner or later, she would find out about Liam.

I was still upset with her for calling Bernard grotesque, but I couldn't let her know. I didn't want to risk it. Just having her beside me made me feel three inches taller and vastly prettier as we entered the lunchroom.

Alejandra and Jana were already seated at our usual table. When Sydney and I joined them, Alejandra switched sides of the table to be closer to me. Jana crossed her arms over her chest and made a huff of disgust. "Ditched *again*," she muttered. Obviously, she was sour at me for not sitting with her on the bus.

"What did I miss?" Sydney asked. Her eyes darted around the circle. She hated being the last to know something.

"Nothing," I mumbled at the exact same time Alejandra asked, "How's your pig?"

"You have a *pig*?" Jana asked incredulously.

Suddenly, all eyes were on me, and Sydney seemed oddly annoyed by it. Her lips drew tight, and her brows slanted downward. But only for a second. As I struggled to untie my tongue, Sydney garnered the table's attention. "The pig's name is Bernard," she said. "Can you believe it? Grace's stepdad gave him to her for Christmas."

There was a moment of quiet while this information was absorbed and while I held my breath. I think Sydney was waiting for the group response before she tipped her hand. Would they laugh or be disgusted the way she was? Would they oink at my expense?

But then Alejandra chimed in, "He's super cute." And I felt a wave of gratitude toward her.

"Really?" Jana asked.

"Really," Alejandra said. "I saw him with Grace at the pet store over break."

Jana didn't look convinced, and Sydney seemed to be watching this exchange with great interest. Something dark passing behind her eyes made me tense. I thought she was going to counter Alejandra's claim with her own "grotesque" assessment of Bernard. But she didn't. Not quite anyway. She batted her eyes at me sweetly and said, "Poor Grace. She really wanted a dog. But her new stepdad is, like, the worse gift giver ever, so I guess it could've been worse, like a snake or something."

The thing was, she wasn't saying anything that I hadn't thought myself. But I didn't like it coming from her mouth.

"Well, I think the pig is amazing," Alejandra said. Beneath the table, she tapped my foot encouragingly with her own. I perked up just in time to catch Sydney's face twitch. It was like she wanted me to be pitied. Like she didn't want me to have something that someone else admired.

Then she smirked and abruptly changed the subject. "Did anyone else notice Coach Fallaci's new haircut in PE?" she asked. "I think his barber must've slipped."

Our teachers lectured all the way through the two after-noon classes Sydney and I had together, so I wasn't able to talk to her again until school was over for the day. She was waiting for me by my locker. Typically, I found her at hers, but I was running a few minutes late and she must've grown impatient.

"What's going on with you?" she asked.

"I don't know. What do you mean?"

"Well, for starters, what were you doing over winter break? I didn't see you at all except for art class." She said this in an exaggeratedly pouty voice.

"My mom had to leave town for work. I didn't do much of anything," I said. The last part wasn't exactly true, but what was I supposed to say? I'd spent most of my days off at a retirement community with a bunch of old people, my pig, and Liam. I knew she wouldn't understand.

My answer seemed to satisfy her a little. Since I didn't own a phone, my mom usually contacted her mom so the two of us could hang out together. With my mom gone, and us living farther apart, it made it difficult to get in touch while my mom was traveling. She knew that.

Still, I could've tried harder to see my best friend. I could've asked Mr. Pine to arrange something, but I hadn't. Why not? Maybe because I'd enjoyed the time I'd spent with Francis and Liam more than the time I'd spent with her. The realization surprised me, but it was true.

"And why did you ride next to Liam Rossi on the bus this morning? Did you not see his hideous backpack?"

So she'd heard about that. I dodged her first question and said, "The backpack isn't that bad. His younger siblings gave it to him."

"That doesn't mean he has to bring it to school. He's a total weirdo."

My skin prickled. I was nervous to contradict Sydney and anxious she'd ditch me because she didn't like who I was hanging out with. But I'd gotten to know Liam over break, and he'd become my friend. I had to defend him. "No," I said firmly. "He's nice."

"Nice?"

I didn't like the way the word left her mouth. It sounded like a hiss. "Yes, nice," I said, then gritted my teeth. My nervousness was quickly morphing into annoyance, and I was having a hard time biting it back.

"Don't you remember how he acted at my Halloween party?" she shot back. "He practically ruined it just by being there."

I'd forgotten about Sydney's party. Two years ago, when we'd been in fourth grade, Sydney's mom had made her invite our entire class—which was the only reason Liam was there. He showed up in some type of *Star Wars* costume. It had gills, and everyone said he looked like a giant fish. So he curled his fingers inside his mouth, like he was on a hook. Then he flopped around the room as if he were being reeled in by an unseen fisherman.

Jana had come to Sydney's party dressed as a cat. Her tail was connected to the back of her costume with an invisible string. When she walked, the tail swayed with her. While Liam was acting like a fish on a hook, he accidently snagged Jana's tail and ripped it loose from her costume.

"He didn't tear Jana's costume on purpose," I said, "and he felt awful about it." He'd apologized profusely.

"That's not my point," Sydney said. "If Liam had just acted like a normal human being, it never would've happened. And if you start hanging out with someone like that, everyone will make assumptions about you. Then you won't be invited to go anywhere, just like no one wants to invite Liam to anything because they're afraid he'll start acting like a fish again or a bug or who knows what."

While Sydney was talking, I remembered something else about that night. Jana was so upset because her mom had *made* her costume. Jana had called her, and her mom came to the rescue and stitched it back together before we went trick-or-treating. I bet her mom could sew just about anything. *Even a cape and a little top hat.* I couldn't believe my luck. Securing a costume was the first step and of utmost importance when it came to turning Bernard into a therapy pig.

"Well, are you?" Sydney asked.

"Am I what?" At some point, I'd stopped listening to my

best friend, and I hadn't even noticed she was still talking.

"I said, 'Are you going to start acting all weird, too?'"

"Of course not," I answered absently, still thinking about Jana's mom. Maybe she could help me. If I hurried, I might even be able to catch Jana before she left for the day and find out.

"Good, because I think we should talk about—"

Sydney had that look about her like she was gearing up for one of her long-winded speeches. She liked to talk, and she liked me to listen, but I didn't have time to stick around and hear what she had to say. So I did something I rarely did, and I interrupted her. "I'm sorry, Syd. I've got to go!"

"Grace? What do you think you're doing?" she said as I stepped deeper into the hallway and was engulfed by the current of middle schoolers flowing out of the building.

"I have to find Jana before she leaves and ask her about a top hat and cape for my pig!" I shouted, and a few heads quizzically turned my direction.

Sydney smiled sweetly at a cute soccer player walking by before returning her attention to me and sneering, "Yeah, 'cause that's not weird at all."

Hoping she didn't see me flinch, I pretended not to hear her as I set off in search of Jana. The costume was too important. There weren't many things that I'd bolt on Sydney for, but this was one of them.

Pig heart valves are sometimes used to replace human heart valves.

I had to ask four people if they'd seen Jana before one of them pointed me in the direction of the theater room. When I found her, she was seated cross-legged on the edge of the stage, reading a script.

"Uh, Jana," I said.

She paused long enough to glance up at me and then went back to reading. The cover of the script read *The Princess and the Pauper.*

"Are you trying out for the spring play?" I asked. I'd seen posters in the hallway. The auditions were today.

"Does that surprise you?" There was a chill to her voice that made me wince.

"Yes," I said. "I mean no. I just thought you wouldn't have time with dance and all."

"I'm trying something new. So what," she said dismissively.

"That's cool," I said. It made sense, really. In dance she performed on a stage, and in a play, she would also be performing on a stage. "You'll be great!" I said, and I meant it.

That seemed to soften her a little, but I could tell she was still feeling salty at me for ditching her on the bus earlier. "Why are you here?" she asked.

"Ah, well, I want to ask a favor . . ."

She blinked at me. "Okay."

I took a deep breath to steady myself. I never had liked asking for help. But I thought Bernard would be so irresistibly cute in costume that my mom and Mr. Pine couldn't help but see his potential as a joy-spreading therapy pig and all-around-wonderful family pet. "Does your mom still sew?" I asked when I'd finally worked up the nerve.

"Yes."

"Do you think . . . do you think, she could make a top hat and a cape for me?"

Jana raised her eyebrows. "Why? Are you thinking of taking up magic?"

"They're not for me. I mean they are, but they're for my pig to wear."

Jana stifled a laugh. "You're serious?"

"Dead serious."

"Well, I have a ton of outfits I've worn to dance recitals. I bet my mom could alter one to fit your pig. Piece of cake."

"That would be incredible!" I wanted to hug Jana, but she was too far elevated above me on the stage. "How much do you think she'd charge?" I asked, worried I might not be able to afford her mom's services.

Jana cocked her head. "You really have a pig?"

"A real live honest-to-goodness pig."

"Is he tame?"

"Completely," I said with confidence. "He can sit, shake, twirl, and honk a horn."

Jana considered my words carefully. "Then you won't have to pay my mom a dime. I know she'll happily do it for free—that is, *if* you loan me your pig."

"If I *what*?"

"Come with me." Jana hopped off the stage and landed with all the grace of an accomplished dancer a foot in front of me. I followed her into the wings and right up to Ms. Stewart, the theater teacher. Ms. Stewart had short pink-tinged hair and a colorful scarf floating loosely around her neck.

"Ms. Stewart," Jana said sweetly. "I noticed that the pauper in the script is a poor country girl."

"That's right, Jana."

"Do you think she might have a pig?" Jana asked.

"I suppose she might," Ms. Stewart said. "I'm almost afraid to ask, but why do you want to know?" Some teachers were putty in Jana's hands, the same way they were in Sydney's. But Ms. Stewart was too sharp to be manipulated. Or so I thought.

"I just thought that maybe, if I got the part of the pauper, I could bring in a real pig. You know, to make the play seem more atmospheric."

I'd already suspected what Jana was up to, but this confirmed it. She was using my pig as a bargaining chip to get the role she wanted. She would get me the costume, and in exchange, Bernard and I would help her become a pauper. I just hoped I wasn't promising her something I couldn't deliver. Opening night was far beyond the trial period.

"To be honest with you, Jana, I'd pictured you in the role of the princess, not the pauper," Ms. Stewart said. I didn't say it, but I agreed with the theater teacher. Jana was far more glitz and glamour than rags and, well, pigs.

Jana's smile strained. "I'm tired of giving people what they expect from me."

Ms. Stewart looked pleasantly surprised. "Okay, then," she

said. "Nail the audition first, but I think your chances are good and a pig would definitely add a little pizzazz to the show."

. . .

I was floating on clouds as I left the school building. Jana had promised to ask her mom about a costume for Bernard that night. There was a good chance it would be finished by the time Mom and Mr. Pine returned from their trip, and well within the trial period. I could only imagine the response Bernard would get from them and at the retirement community when he strutted into the garden in his cape and top hat. Francis would be over the moon. He would agree to be my co-handler and everything else would fall into place.

I was in such a state thinking about it that I started walking home—to my *old* apartment. I was a block away from school when I realized I was traveling in the wrong direction. Worse, I'd missed the bus!

It wasn't the first time I'd forgotten I was on a tight schedule after school. After years of wandering around at my leisure after the last bell, it hadn't been an easy adjustment. But those times, I'd called Mom from the front office. The last time it happened, she'd sent Mr. Pine to retrieve me, and I could tell it hadn't made him happy. I'd sworn not to let it happen again. Yet here I was.

My heartbeat flooded my ears. Neither Mom nor Mr. Pine could come to my rescue now. I weighed my options. I could walk. If all went well, I would arrive home in an hour or so. But I'd have to cross a state highway, and if Mom ever found out, she'd kill me—that is if I wasn't flattened by a semi first. Emma had made it clear she wasn't my taxi service the day she'd given me and Bernard a ride to the vet. Not to mention I wasn't eager to let her know I'd messed up *or* get back in a car with her behind the wheel. I had Sydney's number memorized. But I dismissed that idea nearly as quickly as I dismissed calling Emma.

The school was practically deserted, but I knew at least one person still on the premises. I decided to wait for Jana to finish her audition. She was onstage when I found my way back into the theater.

The room was dark except for the stage lights, and only a few seats near the front were filled. Jana was holding a basket and pretending to peddle some flowers. The look on her face was remarkably humble. It struck me that she really was a decent actress. Ms. Stewart seemed pleased with the performance as well. She clapped loudly from the front row when Jana was finished.

I forgot myself and started clapping loudly, too—from the *back* of the theater. When the ten or so students in the front row turned and scowled at me, I wished I hadn't. I don't think they thought I was obnoxious for clapping, the way Sydney would've. It was just that the theater kids all hung together. Jana's sudden interest had to be unsettling enough. The two of us combined must've seemed like an infiltration.

"Will you be auditioning for a role, too, Grace?" Ms. Stewart asked.

"Me, um, no." I scurried forward toward the stage to meet Jana as she walked down the side steps.

"What do you want now?" she whispered impatiently as Sarah Nguyen took the stage.

"Could I maybe get a ride?" While I shifted my weight from one foot to the other, I told her how I'd missed the bus and that I couldn't call my mom because she was out of town.

Jana seemed annoyed. If I'd known this morning that I'd be asking her for not one but two favors, I would've sat next to her on the way to school. On second thought, that wasn't true. I still would've ridden next to Liam.

"Fine," she said.

After that, things unfolded rather quickly. Since Jana had completed her audition, she was free to leave. We walked directly to the parking lot, where Jana's mom was waiting in a sleek metallic-silver sedan. Jana leaned in the car window and explained that I needed a ride and then proceeded to ask her mom if she could also alter one of Jana's dance outfits for me.

Jana's mom not only agreed, she also said we could swing by their house to pick the costume up and then proceed to my house for measurements.

Next thing I knew, we were on the road, and Jana's mom was asking, "Which dance company are you joining?"

"Who, me?" I ask, momentarily confused before realizing that Jana hadn't clarified what I'd be using the costume for. "Oh, no, I'm not dancing. The costume is for my pig."

The car swerved almost imperceptibly before Jana's mom regained her composure. "Oh, really . . . okay, that's unusual." Her response made me uneasy, but at least she didn't back out.

We swung by their house to pick up the old tap dance costume. I'd never seen Jana's house before. It was bigger than Sydney's, with two large brick columns in the front, enough garage doors for three houses, and a ridiculously well-manicured yard with stone paths and a water feature in front. It was certainly not the home of a pauper, and it made me second-guess my decision to ask them for a ride. Granted, Mr. Pine's house was a whole lot nicer than our old apartment. Still, I now dreaded the thought of her and her mom seeing the cracks in our cement driveway, peeling paint, and ragged carpets when they lived in a home straight out of a magazine.

I nervously waited in the car with Jana's mom while Jana ran in to retrieve the outfit.

"Aren't you Sydney's friend?" her mom asked when we were alone. She sized me up in her rearview mirror.

I thought it was a strange question. "Yes, *and* Jana's," I answered.

"Right. Of course," Jana's mom said. "I just meant that you're the girl Sydney's mom babysat for years."

"That's me," I said brightly, even though on the inside I was boiling. Jana's mom was starting to make me feel like a charity case. I eyed her expensive purse, her flawless skin, and her perfectly painted fingernails drumming the steering wheel of her Mercedes, and I realized she was trying to understand why her daughter was hanging out with someone like me. Someone a little awkward. Someone with a tattered backpack and a bargain-salon haircut. She was looking at me the same way Sydney always looked at Liam. Like I was less than.

I shrunk back into the leather seat, wishing I could altogether disappear.

Thankfully, Jana was in and out lickety-split, and we were back on our way. When we arrived at Mr. Pine's house, I almost told Jana's mom to forget the whole thing. I didn't want a favor from someone who looked down her nose at me.

But I wanted that costume more.

As we entered the house, I scrambled to snatch and crumple up a few of Mr. Pine's haphazard sticky notes. There was one stuck to the back of the couch and another in the hallway leading into the kitchen.

Jana's family struck me more as the type that would have fine art hanging on their walls—not squares of bright yellow paper. I didn't look back until we were all the way through the house and to the garage access door in the kitchen. I didn't think I could bear to see the expressions on my visitors' faces.

Yet, when I was brave enough to peek, Jana smiled at me warmly and the expression on her mom's face was pleasant enough. Was it possible they hadn't noticed the shambles? Was the condition of our home not as embarrassing as I'd thought? Maybe they were just being polite. But then I swung open the door to the garage and Jana's mom gasped when she saw Bernard. "Oh my!" she said.

My cheeks burned at the same time Bernard grunted. I'd noticed that his greeting grunt was individualized to the person. When he greeted me, his grunt was almost singsongy. It was more a contented grumble for Emma, and for Liam and Francis, it was deep and low, like he was trying to appear more manly in their presence.

At first, Bernard's grunt sounded as it usually does when I came near. But our guest's alarm made him uneasy, and it turned squealy and high. I rushed to comfort him. "It's all right,

Bernard." I gently scratched behind his ear, near his kidney-shaped spot and made shushing noises until the squealing stopped.

"I'm sorry," Jana's mom muttered. "It's just that I thought, well, I thought he would be smaller. More teacup-sized. Teacup pigs are in vogue, you know. Celebrities keep them as pets. So I assumed your pig would also be tiny and cute."

There was a lot to unpack in that statement. I was surprised she thought I had anything in common with celebrities. But maybe she couldn't fathom anyone not living a life based on what was or wasn't "in vogue." And then there was her reaction to his size. It was almost as bad as Sydney calling him grotesque. Why did some people think something could only be cute if it was small?

"Mom," Jana said cuttingly, and I could tell she felt bad about her mother's snooty reaction.

"Actually," I said, "there's no such thing as a 'teacup pig.' It's just a name some greedy breeders use to mislead buyers and trick them into purchasing a pig that won't stay small forever anyway. Sometimes the breeders are even cruel and starve the pigs to stunt their growth."

"That's awful," Jana said. Then she turned to her mother and with laser sharpness added, "Imagine having to starve yourself to stay skinny and small." Something about the way she said it made me think she was speaking from experience. That made me sad for her.

Jana's mom smiled a little too sweetly and said, "Well, we should probably get started."

I commanded Bernard to stay while Jana's mom used a ribbon tape to measure around his neck and down his back. And then she placed Jana's old top hat on his head. It was shiny and black and just a tad crooked. It flattened one of his large pointy ears and complemented his fleshy pink skin nicely. I nearly lost it; he looked so ridiculously cute. Then he wriggled his snout, and even Jana said, "Aww."

Somehow, though, Jana's mom remained unaffected. "I'll have to add an elastic strap, something comfortable to wrap under his neck to hold it in place," she said. "But it should work, and the cape will hardly need any adjusting. I should have the alterations finished in a day or two, and I'll send it to school with Jana."

Despite feeling snubbed by Jana's mom, I was full of gratitude. "Thank you so much," I said sincerely. I couldn't wait for Mom and Mr. Pine to see Bernard in costume—I knew it would make him irresistible. And even before then, when he wore it to his grand reappearance at the retirement community, Francis was going to flip.

14

**Pigs are surprisingly fast runners. An adult pig
can run a mile in seven minutes.**

ernard had been sleeping in my room every night, on his
pile of blankets in the corner. That evening, he clambered
into bed with me soon after I'd fallen asleep. There's nothing quite like being startled awake by a seventy-five-pound ball of
lard. But I made room, and he snuggled in quickly. Long after he
had drifted off, I lay there enjoying the comfort of his soft, warm
piggy self nestled near me and listening to the sound of his rhythmic snores. The last thought I had before falling back asleep was
that my plan couldn't fail. Mom and Mr. Pine had to see how
amazing Bernard was, and soon. The trial period was more than
halfway over, and my heart would shatter if I had to give him up.

I hadn't seen Emma at all the evening before. She'd been
gone when Jana and her mom brought me home and must've

returned after I'd gone to bed. She'd used Mr. Pine's sticky notes to lay claim to the leftovers in the fridge, so I'd been forced to make myself a peanut butter and jelly sandwich for dinner. Which wasn't enough.

My stomach was growling when I awoke. Or was it Bernard's stomach? He was so close to me it was difficult to tell precisely where the grumbling was coming from. I nudged him gently, and he grunted back at me. I'd made the exact same noise when Mom had tried to wake me for the first day of school after a summer of sleeping in. I blew softly on the back of his ears. He grunted again. "Come on, sleepyhead, wake up," I said. When he still refused to stir, I climbed over his massive body and found my way to the kitchen.

Emma was already seated at the table. She glowered at me from above her cereal bowl, then went back to staring at something on her phone. She thought I was the spoiled one, yet she had not only a phone but a car as well.

"Good morning to you, too," I said grumpily, and grabbed the Cheerios box from the counter. Ever since I'd started training Bernard, I'd avoided eating Cheerios myself, in addition to all pork products. But this morning, it was the O-shaped cereal or nothing.

We ate our breakfast in silence. I was nearly down to the last O floating in my milk when a loud crash rang out from somewhere deeper inside the house. Emma and I made eye contact for a split second. Then we both leaped from our chairs and raced down the hall.

At the door to her room, Emma screeched to a halt in front of me. Peeking around her, all I could see was a wagging pink tail and total destruction. "Get your pig out of here, now!" she bellowed.

Bernard had rummaged through her trash and somehow upended everything on Emma's dresser. Mostly that meant used tissues, lotion bottles, makeup containers, and brushes strewn across the floor. But he'd also knocked down picture frames, and at least one of them, a porcelain frame with delicate roses, was lying in pieces at the base of her bed. It was the same frame I'd seen her holding while she was crying.

I couldn't make eye contact with my stepsister. "Bernard," I called. "Come!"

Bernard obediently turned tail and trotted out of Emma's room while she shot straight for the broken frame. As Bernard rubbed against my legs, grunting his happy hello, she clutched what was left of the frame to her chest.

I couldn't see the front of the frame, or the photo inside it, but obviously it was important to her. I suspected the photo was of someone she had loved and lost. "Emma, I'm really sorry," I said.

The look she gave me in return was a mixture of anger and

agony. "Why was Bernard left alone inside the house?"

"I—He—" I stammered. "I was hungry, but he was asleep, and I couldn't wake him."

"So once again, you were only thinking about yourself."

"That's not true," I protested.

"Just take your pig and go. I don't want to see either of your ugly faces right now. In fact, I'd rather not see them *ever*."

I recoiled as much for Bernard as for me. It had been clear from the day Emma moved in that she loathed me, but she'd never said so much as one cruel word about my pig. "Is that right? Well, I'm *glad* your stupid nose hole closed up!" I shot back.

I admit, it wasn't a terrific comeback. But it was the best I could do at the moment, and apparently it was enough to send her over the edge. "You're what?" she screeched. She snatched a hairbrush from the floor and hurled it straight at me.

I ducked, and the brush bounced off the wall behind me. It clattered to the floor. "Come on," I said to Bernard, and retreated down the hallway before her aim improved.

My anger was like fire, hot and consuming. But dread quickly doused the flame. I halted in my tracks, and Bernard rammed into the back of my knees, causing me to stumble. How was I supposed to convince Mom and Mr. Pine to keep Bernard now that Emma hated not just me but him as well? Even if I succeeded in turning Bernard into the world's best therapy animal, I worried it wouldn't be enough.

A crushing wave of regret for leaving Bernard unsupervised washed over me. As if I wasn't under enough pressure to please everyone—to be the perfect stepdaughter, the perfect pet owner, the perfect friend—this slipup would make it immeasurably more difficult to win over my stepsister. And she already seemed to hold the very fact that I was alive against me.

Bernard softly snuffled me with his snout, and I felt the warmth of his breath even through my jeans. I leaned back and scratched behind his ear. "I know you didn't mean to cause any trouble," I said. "I just hope Mr. Pine will see it that way, too."

I resumed leading him through the house and out into the garage, where he'd be out of Emma's line of fire and hopefully wouldn't cause any more damage. After getting him settled with everything he'd need while I was at school, I left as quickly as possible. Leaving early meant a longer wait at the bus stop. But even though I was a shivering blue Popsicle by the time the bus arrived, it was better than being pelted with beauty supplies or turning to frost under Emma's glacier stare.

Once I stepped aboard the bus and began to thaw, both Liam and Jana gazed at me expectantly. Each had an open spot right beside them. I shot Liam an apologetic look as I slid in next to Jana. She smiled triumphantly. I shrunk in my seat. I hadn't chosen Jana because I wanted to sit by her any more than I did

Liam. It was that, considering the favor she was doing for me and Bernard, I felt I owed it to her. Plus, I was starting to think she was more complex than I'd ever given her credit for.

It was weird. For years, I'd felt tied to Sydney and never really had to choose between friends. Many things had been changing, though, since Christmas morning, when Bernard arrived. As soon as the bus rumbled to a start, I glanced around the seat, back a few rows to where Liam was sitting. He caught my gaze and smiled, and I breathed a little more freely. He wasn't upset.

"My mom almost has Bernard's costume finished already," Jana said, drawing my focus back to her.

"That's great! Thank you," I said. "So when do you find out if you get to play the pauper?"

"Today," Jana said. "I'm really nervous. I have butterflies in my stomach and everything."

Jana did look worried. I was surprised. She didn't seem like the type of person who'd felt insecure for a single moment of her life. "Don't sweat it," I said. "Shockingly, you make an excellent pauper."

Jana beamed. "You think so?"

"Yeah, I do." For the rest of the bus ride, we talked about the play and about Bernard and the topic of dance didn't come up once. If it had, though, I don't think I would've minded. Maybe the main reason Jana had only ever talked to me about dance was we just hadn't had anything else to talk about. But now we did.

As we shuffled off the bus, I told her I couldn't wait to hear if she got the part. Several times during my morning classes, I found myself feeling nervous on her behalf and wondering if she'd heard anything yet.

Then, at lunch, I was the first person she ran to in the cafeteria. Before I could take a seat at our usual table, she was in front of me, grasping my arms and screaming, "I got it! I got it!"

I found myself swooped up in her excitement and bouncing off the floor with her in celebration. "Congratulations!" I said. "I can't wait to see you in the play! Does this mean that Bernard has a part, too?"

Jana grinned. "Yes, I mean only if you want. I'll ask my mom to finish the alterations regardless. I have a ton of old dance outfits. We're happy one of them will be used again."

"Thanks," I said, "but I think Bernard is a born showman. He's in all the way!"

"Good," said Jana. "I was hoping you'd say that."

As we took our seats at the table, I realized that something had shifted between us. Yesterday, the favor had been a bargaining tool. Now she was offering to do it with no strings attached. Why? I'd ridden next to her on the bus for months because we were both friends with Sydney, not because either of us thought we had that much in common. And we were still very different people, but that was okay. And maybe that's what was needed for us to truly be friends all along—just being okay with our differences.

I was still buzzing with joy, so I almost didn't notice the stony expression on Sydney's face. *Almost.* Her lips were drawn in a narrow line, and I nearly knocked over my milk box—her glare was that unnerving. But whatever it was passed quickly. One minute she was ice; the next she was fawning all over Jana. "Of course you got it! Ms. Stewart would be an idiot not to cast you in any role you wanted." She then proceeded to drill Jana with a thousand questions about the play. It was unusual for her to spend so much time and energy pressing for details about something other than middle school gossip. At first, I thought she must really be interested in the school production of *The Princess and the Pauper*.

But when she didn't so much as glance in my direction, not even once for the entire lunch period, I knew something was wrong. She was mad at me. Earlier that morning, Bernard and I had gotten even further on Emma's bad side, and now I was in a giant hole with Sydney, too. I hadn't spoken with Sydney since I'd bolted on her to find Jana the day before. But thanks to our weekly art class, we'd be spending an hour together after school. I told myself that when it was just the two of us, it'd be harder for her to ignore me. When it was just the two of us, things would be okay again. At least, I hoped they would.

15

Reaching up to 130 decibels, a pig's squeal can be louder than a jet engine.

The art center was only a few blocks away from the middle school. Before Mom went on vacation, she arranged for Sydney's mom to give me a ride home. But the plan had been for me and Sydney to walk to the class together.

I looked everywhere for Sydney after the final bell rang. At my locker, at hers. I asked Alejandra which direction she'd gone, since the two of them had seventh period together. Alejandra said she was pretty sure she'd seen Sydney exiting the building.

I didn't want to leave without her if Alejandra was mistaken. So I paced back and forth under the flagpole until the halls were empty and the sea of kids thinned out completely and it was clear that Sydney was already gone.

Seeds of doubt festered in my mind as I speedwalked the

few blocks to the center. Was she really that upset with me, or had Sydney forgotten about our class altogether? What if I was stuck without a ride home again? Worse, what if she was sick or something bad had happened to her? But there she was, seated right at our table the moment I walked in. She'd gotten an early start finishing the project we'd begun the previous week. She was absorbed with painting a layer of decoupage glue on the woven paper and adhering it to a wooden frame.

I clenched my jaw as I approached the table. It was bad enough that she'd ignored me all through lunch, but ditching me after school, too, when we were supposed to walk here together? I'd wanted so badly for things to be okay between us, but I'd gotten all worked up on the way here, and then to find her acting so nonchalant—well, I was fire-cracker hot and angry. "Hey," I said pointedly.

She glanced up, then went back to working on her frame.

I wasn't about to let her off that easy. "Why did you leave me behind?"

"Oh, you mean like you ditched me after school yesterday."

"That was different," I said defensively. "I needed to find Jana. It was important."

"Yeah, I can tell the two of you are all buddy-buddy now. Same with you and Alejandra and you and Liam. Pretty much the only person you're not acting like a friend to these days is me," she snapped. "And *I'm* supposed to be your best friend, Grace."

"You are my best friend."

"So start behaving like it," she said.

I didn't know how to respond to that. In my mind, I hadn't done anything to make her think otherwise. Not only that, I wasn't used to having to defend myself with Sydney. We'd hardly ever fought. I grabbed my supplies and sat down next to her. Neither of us said anything until the earthy colors of my frame reminded me of Francis and his unusual occupations, and I wanted to say something, anything, to break the uncomfortable silence. "Did you know that some people pick worms for a career, and that a pig can smell something as deep as twenty-five feet underground?"

Sydney stared at me like I'd grown a third eye. "Why are you telling me this?"

"I don't know." I shrugged. "Because it's interesting?"

"Is it?" she asked in a way that made it clear it very much wasn't. Not to her at least. What I didn't say was that I'd wanted to see how she'd react. Insects were Liam's thing and pigs were starting to be mine, and I guess I'd been testing her. I'd wanted to see if she was open to hearing about stuff I wanted to talk about, or if she'd shut me down if I wanted to discuss things that she cared nothing about.

Not that I was surprised, but she shut me down all the way. She stared at me until I dropped my head in submission, and she no doubt felt certain she'd gotten her point across. Then she said, "So I was thinking . . . Why don't you spend the night on Friday? Your mom and stepdad will still be on vacation, right? You can walk home from school with me, and it'll be just like before. We'll stay up late and gorge on popcorn and soda. It'll be *so* much fun." Sydney's whole attitude had changed on a dime. She was chirpy and smiley and nearly impossible to say no to. But I couldn't risk leaving Bernard in Emma's care while I was at Sydney's. Plus, whenever I spent the night at my best friend's house, we stayed up late. Very late. We also slept in the next day. I had big plans for Saturday morning. It would be my first chance to ask Francis about being my co-handler. It couldn't wait. Especially now that Emma had turned on Bernard. The costume would help. However, him looking irresistibly cute might not be enough to counter his destructive streak. I had to have something more to present to Mom and Mr. Pine before Emma broke the news about him wrecking her room. I had to have plans for Bernard and me to continually make a positive impact on not just our family, but the world. Even that might not be enough. Still I had to do everything within in my power. I couldn't lose Bernard over a sleepover.

"I would love to, but I can't. I'm sorry," I said quietly.

"Oh. I see," Sydney said, and immediately turned all silent and sulky again.

With her giving me the cold shoulder, I focused intently on my project. But I didn't stop thinking about our friendship. Not that long ago, I'd felt like I could tell Sydney everything. Now I felt guarded every time I spoke to her. I knew she'd respond to anything I had to say about Francis and the retirement community the same way she had when I showed her the picture of Bernard, and the way she had just a few minutes ago when I'd mentioned worm pickers and how a pig has an outstanding sense of smell. At first, I thought she was different. She never used to respond to me that way. Other people, yes, but not me.

I dipped my sponge brush in the bottle of glue and applied another coat to my frame while thinking, *It wasn't Sydney who had changed*. I was the one who was different. Ever since Bernard had come into my life, my world had been expanding. The reason I was saying and doing things Sydney didn't like was because I'd made new friends and I'd learned things I hadn't known before—about myself and about pigs and people, and so much more.

As the woven paper bonded to the frame, I couldn't believe the difference it made. The unfinished wood had been sturdy but dull. The woven paper was pretty but far too flimsy. Joining the two resulted in a frame that was both beautiful and strong.

It hit me that maybe that was how healthy relationships

were supposed to work. Sydney was agitated by my new friends and interests, because in all the years we'd been friends up until now, I'd only ever tried to be exactly like her. I'd only focused on her interests and limited myself to saying the things I knew she wanted to hear—like how cute her clothes were and how much I loved her favorite music and movies. I never realized it before, but trying to be just like her hadn't done our friendship any favors. Our friendship hadn't been strengthened or made more beautiful by our differences. It made me regret not ever being myself with her. Now I wondered if it was too late.

The rest of class was really awkward as we finished up our frames in silence. Mine turned out way better than I expected. And I knew I wasn't just being biased. When the art teacher held mine up for the rest of the class to see and remarked on how beautifully it had come together, Sydney prickled. I barely noticed, though, because I was busy wondering if Emma would think the frame was good enough to replace the one Bernard had broken. I suspected that no frame could ever be as special to my stepsister as the one she'd lost. Sentimental value and all that. And, obviously, it couldn't come close to replacing the person whose photo had been held in the frame. Still, giving her the one I made felt like the right thing to do. I'd just have to pick a good time to present it to her. The wrong moment, and I might wind up arming her with more ammunition to throw at me.

The ride home Sydney's mom gave me wasn't any more comfortable than art class. No doubt Sydney was still agitated, and that's why she wasn't speaking to me. I wasn't annoyed at Sydney, though; I was just sad. Really sad. I'd always assumed Sydney and I would be best friends forever. Now I wasn't so sure.

Her mom's eyes kept darting between us. I could tell by the expression on her face that she didn't know what to make of the rift between Sydney and me. I thought I knew why we'd barely ever fought in all the years we'd been friends. It's hard to disagree with someone who mirrors your tastes and opinions. But maybe a little more disagreement would've been good for us. Maybe an argument now and then would've strengthened our bond.

Despite everything, I wasn't ready to give up all hope that our friendship could survive. Even though I'd made new friends, she was the strongest connection I had—we'd been close for so long. And I was nervous about what school would be like without her. I'd always been "Sydney's best friend." Would people still like me when I was just Grace?

When her mom stopped the car in front of my house, I asked Sydney if she wanted to come inside. "You can meet my pig," I offered tentatively. I thought Bernard would win her over, but I also worried she might insult him again instead.

"We have a few minutes," her mom said helpfully. "I know I'd like to meet him."

Sydney shook her head. "Sorry, we've got to go," she said snidely. "I have too much homework."

"Okay, maybe next time," I said. She didn't respond.

Feeling dejected, I entered Mr. Pine's empty house alone. Even after retrieving Bernard from the garage, the sense of restlessness didn't go away. I was distracted while we worked on skills together in my room. Instead of remaining firm and consistent, I half-heartedly praised him when he did something right and let it go when he didn't respond to my commands.

I couldn't help it. I kept thinking about Sydney and hoping our troubles would just go away. That things would magically go back to normal between the two of us. And yet I sort of hoped they wouldn't. It wasn't worth being best friends with her if I had to give up all the wonderful things that were happening to me. Minus Emma, things had gotten better in so many ways.

When I dropped a tissue on the carpet and Bernard wouldn't "leave it," I gave up for the night. Between fighting with my stepsister and not getting along with Sydney, I really missed Mom. Thank goodness I had Bernard. He didn't have to master every skill right away, did he? For tonight, it was enough to be able to snuggle up with him again as I fell asleep.

The following morning, when I stepped onto the bus, I

motioned to Liam, and he moved a few rows up from his usual spot to a seat right across from Jana and me. That way, we could all ride together.

It wasn't until Jana asked Liam, "Do you?" that I noticed he was wearing his "Eat Bugs, Save the Planet" T-shirt again.

"Do I what?"

"Eat bugs?" Jana's expression was full of revulsion, and I worried I'd made a terrible mistake by bringing them together.

"Nah," Liam said. "But we all might have to someday."

"What do you mean?" Jana asked, sounding even more grossed out.

"Well, the world's population is growing so fast that there are going to be food shortages in our lifetime," Liam said. "Insects are high in protein and more environmentally friendly to raise than cows and other livestock. So in the future we might have to consume cricket burgers and that sort of thing. It'll cut down on harmful ozone gases and make it so more people have enough to eat."

My eyes darted back and forth between them. I held my breath, thinking it was just as Sydney had predicted. People would stop wanting to be around me if I continued to hang out with Liam. I fully expected Jana to stand up and move away from both of us. Instead, she said. "Huh, well, I hope it doesn't come to that. But conservation is cool. I'm all for saving the planet."

I breathed a sigh of relief, and then Jana whipped out Bernard's new costume, and I needed a moment to recover all over again. It was that adorable.

"Nice," Liam said. "Francis is gonna love it."

"I wish he could wear it for the play," Jana said, and giggled. "But it doesn't really make sense for a pig in a fancy outfit to be hanging out with a pauper."

"You're in the school play?" Liam asked. "And Bernard is, too?"

Apparently, *The Princess and the Pauper* was an adaptation of a Mark Twain book called *The Prince and the Pauper*. Liam had read the book, and he and Jana immediately launched into making comparisons between the play and the novel. I never would've guessed that Liam and Jana would have much in common. But despite the bug shirt, they hit it off. As we were exiting the bus, Jana said, "Hey, you should sit with us at lunch. Just don't talk about insects while we're eating. I get that we might all have to eat them someday, but for now I just want to enjoy my pepperoni pizza."

"No problem." Liam grinned. "Thanks."

After third period, I kept an eye out for Sydney on my way to the cafeteria. The way things had ended the day before, my stomach was bursting with butterflies to see her again. Would she link her arm through mine, and all would be forgotten?

Even if she did, I didn't think it'd go over well when she found out Jana had asked Liam to sit at our lunch table.

When I spotted her, she was across the hall with her arm looped through Shreya Bhatti's arm. I didn't know Shreya that well. She'd gone to one of the other elementary schools and had entered middle school with her own circle of friends.

Sydney was shining brightly the way she always did—her smile and laughter infectious. Even though I'd enjoyed the company of my new friends, I'd felt a little gloomier than usual all morning. It hadn't been a bad day. I'd even managed to avoid Emma's scorn before school. But I felt like a tiny piece of my heart was missing. Sydney didn't look like she was being dragged down in the slightest. She'd moved on.

I lumbered toward the table where Alejandra, Jana, and Liam were already seated, knowing full well that Sydney wouldn't be joining us. Sure enough, she crossed the cafeteria and found an open spot at a table with Shreya and her crowd. Who knew? Maybe she'd sit with them for the rest of the school year.

"What's up with Sydney?" Jana asked as I slumped into my seat.

"Sorry, I think it's my fault," I said. It was one thing for Sydney to move on from our friendship, but I didn't want to cost them their friendships with her, too.

I scanned Alejandra's and Jana's faces, wondering if they

were teetering between staying put and jumping ship so they could go join Sydney. They made eye contact with each other. They did not make eye contact with me.

Here we go, I thought. That thing I'd feared—being friendless in middle school (well, nearly so, because I doubted Liam would desert me)—was about to happen. I braced myself for the rejection. But then Alejandra sighed and said, "It's not *your* fault."

"Yeah," Jana chimed in. "Sydney has bossed all of us around for years. And I'm sick of people making choices for me." Jana looked down and to the side, and it hit me that she wasn't just talking about Sydney. The more I thought about it, the more I realized that Jana's mom and Sydney had a lot in common. "Besides, I like you better when you're not Sydney's puppet," Jana added.

"Thanks," I said. But I could tell that for all Jana's and Alejandra's bravado, they were feeling a little unsettled, too. None of us were really sure where we stood without Sydney. No one was going anywhere yet. But the question of whether we'd stick together without her acting like a magnet for all of us had to be on all our minds.

My heartache was still too fresh to see things clearly. In the back of my mind, I was devising ways to win my best friend back. Maybe if I never spoke of Bernard to her again. Or maybe if *I* were the one to jump ship—if I stopped being so friendly with Liam, Jana, and Alejandra—she wouldn't be so angry with me. Maybe having one best friend was worth giving up all the others.

If I stood up that very minute and walked over and sat next to Sydney, it might show her that I was loyal. *She might take me back.* I thought that was what I wanted more than anything, but then I glanced around the table and I couldn't leave.

Liam had been silent since I'd sat down. He was watching me with those intense hazel eyes of his, and I knew I'd feel like a monster if I abandoned him now. Or Jana, or Alejandra. So I sucked in a breath, a small part of me still hoping I could patch things up with Sydney later, and focused on the boy sitting across from me. "I can't wait for Saturday," I said. "I've been working on a new trick with Bernard. I'm teaching him how to bow. I want to surprise Francis with it, and his costume. I thought it might be fitting with his top hat on. Since both are, you know, kinda formal."

Changing the subject seemed to break the ice for all of us. Liam's face, which had been still and watchful, relaxed. Delight kindled and then caught fire in his eyes. "Awesome," he said. "I'll bring the muffins."

"Why do I feel like I'm missing out on a celebration?" Alejandra cooed.

"Same," said Jana. "Plus, I'd really like to see Bernard in my old jazz outfit."

"Really?" I asked. "I mean, you do realize we're talking about going to an old folks' home. It's not like we're going to a funcenter or anything."

"So? I don't have anything better to do on Saturday," Alejandra said.

"Me neither," Jana added. "I'm taking a break from dance for the play, and rehearsals don't start until next week."

"Okay," I said. "Great!" I was thrilled that they wanted to join us. Maybe we didn't need Sydney to keep us glued together. Saturday was going to be even better than I'd imagined. I had a costume for Bernard and the support of friends. Francis wouldn't dream of turning us down. And the more people I had backing me and Bernard, the more likely it would be to get Mom and Mr. Pine on board.

"See how many people love him?" I could say. "He'll be the perfect therapy pig." Emma's grievances against him would pale in comparison. With so much positive energy, we'd have to keep him, and my stepsister would come around eventually. I knew she would. It would all be okay. All the pieces were falling into place.

Or so I thought.

16

The average life expectancy for a miniature potbellied pig is twelve to eighteen years.

I decided to dress Bernard in his costume before we left the house on Saturday morning. I'd tried it on him once already, the day I'd brought it home from school. It was as much a delight seeing him in it again as it had been the first time. His hat tipped to one side, the magnificent black cape flowed over his fleshy pink frame, and the way he held his chin up proudly while he wore the dapper costume—it was all too good.

It even got a rise out of Emma when nothing else all week had. As I paraded Bernard in full regalia through the kitchen, her eyebrows shot up and one corner of her mouth quirked. That was before she caught me looking, at which point her eyes narrowed in disgust. But all it took was one snout wiggle and a quasi smile from the pig, and her cool exterior cracked. I could hear her suppressing a chuckle as Bernard and I left the room. It gave me confirmation that I was on the right path with this therapy pig thing. All I needed was Francis to make a commitment today, and then Bernard and I would be golden.

As my pig and I walked out the front door and down the sidewalk, his cape whirled and whipped around him. Several cars on the street slowed while the drivers rubbernecked to watch him. He was a spectacle, for sure. One that spread joy wherever he went, and I couldn't wait to make it official. Once Bernard and I completed the certification program, I knew Mom and Mr. Pine would be proud of us. How could anyone not be?

I was walking on air, and there was a lightness to Bernard's trot as well. He didn't glue his flat disk nose to the ground, not even once for our entire walk to the retirement community. He seemed as anxious as I was to get there.

I had my Polaroid camera tucked beneath one arm and my other arm out straight as Bernard dragged me along by the leash. He could be surprisingly swift when he wanted to be. As we approached the retirement community, I spotted Alejandra waiting beneath a tree and Jana hopping out of her mom's metallic-silver Mercedes.

Bernard captured their attention immediately, because how could he not? It was fun to watch my friends' reactions. Jana burst into the air, clapping her hands together and squealing (future captain of the high school cheerleading squad that she was). Alejandra cupped her cheeks in her hands and beamed. Even Jana's mom tapped her horn appreciatively.

I thought now would be an appropriate time to bust out a little preview of the trick we'd practiced for Francis. Bernard bowed on command, while I gave a quick, shy curtsy. By the time we'd finished, Jana and Alejandra had swarmed around us. They gushed all over Bernard and his hat and cape, and my heart soared watching them be charmed by my pig.

We continued into the garden together, and there was Liam waiting with his jumbo-sized plastic container of mini blueberry muffins. His smile was crooked, and so was his hair. It was plastered to one side. It appeared that he'd made an attempt to style it today, but it hadn't exactly cooperated. He was wearing a collared shirt buttoned all the way to the top. Unlike everyone else, his gaze went to me before it went to my pig.

I took a moment to smile back at him and then asked, "Where's Francis?"

Liam shrugged. "He's usually here by now. Maybe he's taking extra time getting dressed for his photo."

"Is that why you're dressed up?" I asked. Liam had never mentioned wanting his portrait taken with Bernard. It pleased me to think that he did.

"Uh . . . yeah . . . it is." He turned a light shade of pink, and I felt bad. I hadn't meant to embarrass him.

But then Jana chimed in, "Oh, can Alejandra and I have our pictures taken, too?" and he surreptitiously breathed a sigh of relief.

"Sure!" I said. "We can take them while we wait for Francis to arrive." By then, I was bursting with nervous energy. Not only did I feel self-conscious about taking my friend's portraits with Liam around (he had more experience), but now that I was here, I felt like I'd die if I had to wait another minute to talk to Francis about the therapy animal certification program.

Jana and Alejandra decided to pose together—kissing Bernard on opposite cheeks as I snapped one Polaroid and then another so they could each have a copy.

For his photo, Liam sat on the bench with Bernard in front of him. Just as I went to snap the picture, Bernard turned his head toward Liam, and Liam glanced down so that they were gazing into each other's eyes. It was the perfect moment to capture on film. And it made me more fully understand what Liam had meant about using photography to tell stories.

While we waited for the images to develop, I tapped my foot impatiently. I couldn't help it. It takes a while, and we had to shield the film from the hazy sunlight. Dark outlines appeared on the blank sheets first, the line of Bernard's cape, Alejandra's sleek black hair, then details and color emerged until, at last, everything came into focus.

Jana and Alejandra were ecstatic about their photos. But the one of Liam and Bernard was my favorite of all the Polaroid photos I'd ever taken. Bernard in his top hat and Liam in his neatly buttoned shirt—they both looked slightly uncomfortable but also gratified, like it was worth it. Like they understood each other and that sometimes it took going outside what you normally did to make something feel special.

I must've hesitated when I went to hand the picture over to Liam, because he said, "You can keep it, if you want." His tone was low and bashful.

"Thank you," I said. I carefully tucked it inside my jacket pocket. I very much did want to keep it. "Where do you think Francis is?"

"I don't know," he said, worry creeping into his voice. "He should be out here by now."

Liam and I paced back and forth and kept our eyes plastered to the front door of the retirement community building. Meanwhile Jana and Alejandra delighted themselves with making Bernard perform for Cheerios. That was until Jana said, "We should probably go. We've been here a while and my mom's waiting in the car to give us a ride home."

"Yeah, no problem," I said a tad too cheerfully.

"Here, take a mini muffin with you," Liam offered, popping the lid off the plastic container.

"Yes, please!" Alejandra said, and snatched one off the top.

"I like him!" Jana stated, and tipped her head toward Liam, while also reaching in to grab a baked good.

Before I could stop myself, I said, "Yeah, me too." But Jana's statement had sounded bold and flippant. I knew I sounded far too dreamy and sincere. This time, I blushed while Liam tugged at his shirt collar, and Alejandra grabbed my hand and squeezed it for moral support. The next thing I knew, though, she and Jana were walking away, and I was left standing there in awkward silence with Liam. Thank God for Bernard. He pushed his way between us and snorted his demands for affection.

"Sorry, Bernard," I said. "Do you feel neglected?" I scratched behind the only ear accessible beneath his top hat. He closed his eyes and grunted appreciatively.

Liam laughed at the look of ecstasy on Bernard's face, and just like that, the tension was broken.

"Should we check inside for Francis, or something?" I asked. I couldn't believe that he'd forgotten. He'd always been so punctual, but maybe?

"I guess," Liam said, sounding as unsure as I felt. We made our way, following the windy concrete path to the front entrance. The lobby of the retirement community reminded me of the dentist's office. There were lines of chairs and a fish tank on the wall. A woman popped up from behind the front desk when we strolled through the automated doors.

She seemed startled, and it took me a minute to figure out why. She was staring at Bernard the same way Sydney had looked at his photo. Despite the fancy attire, all she saw was a beastly farm animal. "You cannot bring a pig in here!" she said, clearly voicing her disapproval.

I should've known better. Still, it hadn't occurred to me that bringing my pig into the retirement community would be any different from bringing him into someone else's house—which I also would've done without a moment's hesitation. "I'm—I'm sorry," I stammered. The thing was, if Bernard was already a therapy pig, it might not have been an issue. More than ever I longed to talk to Francis so we could get started with the program. Yet I was painfully aware that Bernard and I didn't have the proper certification to be welcomed here. "I'll wait outside with Bernard," I said to Liam. "You go find Francis."

Bernard and I exited the way we'd come as Liam proceeded to the front desk. While I waited by a little dry water feature with rocks but no stream trickling down during these colder winter months, Bernard rubbed against my pant leg. It was like he could sense my unease.

It didn't help any when Liam came ambling out the door

with a bewildered expression on his face. "What is it?" I asked.

"She said they don't have a single resident named Francis."

"What? Are you sure? I . . . I don't understand."

"I don't either," said Liam. "I think she was annoyed. About the pig and us being kids. I don't think she took me seriously, but I don't think she was lying either. Anyway, she told me I had to leave."

"What about Alice and the other residents? They all knew Francis. He has to *live* here," I insisted. "It doesn't make sense." Without Francis, Bernard and I couldn't get certified. When Mom and Mr. Pine returned, I couldn't announce that I'd already started the process—which I knew would've solidified Bernard's place in the family and, in a roundabout way, mine as well. I felt like the ground had tilted sideways and I was free-falling.

"Maybe he told us the wrong name?" Liam said. "You know, how he calls me Bob or Fred or George, but never Liam. Maybe he was doing the same thing, only with himself."

Come to think of it, I hadn't heard any of the other residents call him Francis. I couldn't remember them calling him by any name. "Then how are we supposed to find him?" I swallowed a hard lump in my throat. "How will we know if something bad happened to him?" Guilt engulfed me. My initial response was concern for myself and Bernard. But if Francis was sick or maybe something worse—that would be an even bigger blow.

"I'm not sure," Liam said. He kicked the ground with his toe. "I guess we don't know as much about him as we thought."

More emotions poured into the storm brewing inside me. *Was anything he'd told us true?* His stories about the things he'd done, they'd seemed a little far-fetched, but when it came down to it, I'd believed him. Now I felt betrayed by a friend all over again. I'd thought the retirement community was the one place I could let down my guard and just be myself. But if all along Francis had been pretending to be someone he wasn't, had any of it been real?

I vented my frustration and guilt and sadness and anger with a loud growl-ish scream: "GRRAARGH!"

A couple having a conversation in the parking lot nearby froze and stared. Sydney would've been appalled. Liam didn't seem embarrassed, though. He said, "Yeah, I know. What do you want to do?"

I figured if Francis was going to come out to the gardens today, he would've done so by now. And I was too disheartened to stand around watching people enter and exit the building with little hope of seeing our friend. "I just want to go home," I said.

Liam nodded. "Me too."

17

Pigs are omnivores and have around 15,000 taste buds.
Humans only have 9,000.

It was a rotten Saturday. Nothing had turned out the way I'd planned, and I didn't know what to do with myself. After sulking in my room for a bit, I decided to work on skills with Bernard. As usual, he sailed right through "sit," "come," and "stay," but for the life of me, I couldn't get him to "leave it."

I set a small trash can in the center of my room, which might as well have been a homing beacon for Bernard. As he trotted straight for it, I held a Cheerio out and commanded him to "leave it." But the allure of the trash was too strong. Time after time, he ignored me in favor of burrowing his head through tissues and kitchen remnants.

Finally, I removed the trash can from my room and

collapsed on my bed. "It's pointless," I groaned. Bernard tried his hardest—nudging me with nose snuffles and wagging his tail—but not even he could cheer me up.

I didn't know why I'd been working on skills anyway. Without Francis, there was little chance of turning Bernard into a therapy pig, and I was terrified I wouldn't be able to keep him. Emma was going to railroad me and Bernard when Mom and Mr. Pine returned. My hopes that we'd ever be a happy family were quickly evaporating.

Then there was Sydney. I'd believed that this day—visiting the retirement community with my new friends and starting down the path of certification—was going to paint bright cheerful brushstrokes over the heartache of losing my best friend. Instead, I was in a worse place. A dark place. It felt like all the pieces that had come together in my life since Christmas were starting to fall apart. I didn't know what I could do to stop it.

As I fully sprawled out on my bed, and Bernard wandered off to a pile of blankets in the corner, my fears only compounded. I was simultaneously worried about Francis and frustrated with him for lying to us. Plus, he had been the bond that connected me to Liam. Well, he and Bernard anyway. Without Francis around to lead Bernard's training sessions, would Liam and I remain friends? I sat up and rummaged through my jacket pocket for the photo I'd taken of Bernard and Liam. My heart ached just looking at it. I couldn't bear to give either of them up. I was staring at the photo when Emma knocked on my door. "There's a boy here to see you," she said gruffly.

Bernard, who'd fallen asleep in the corner, opened one eye and grunted drowsily. I shot to my feet. "Liam?" I asked.

"How should I know?" Emma answered through the door. "Just come find out yourself." She'd retreated to her room by the time I entered the hallway.

Bernard clambered to his hooves and followed me to the entryway, where Liam was waiting, shuffling his feet and wringing his hands. He didn't even say hello before blurting out, "He's in the hospital."

"What?"

Words came flowing out of Liam's mouth in one rapid gush. "Francis. Harold. Whatever his name is. I was keeping an eye out my back window, and I saw Alice pushing her hot pink walker through the gardens and I hopped the fence, and anyway, I asked her about Francis and she said his name is really Harold and that he was transported to the hospital yesterday in an ambulance and she doesn't know what's wrong with him, but she thought he was in pretty bad shape and I think maybe we should go see him but my mom has to watch my younger siblings and my dad is out doing deliveries. I thought maybe you had a way to get us there?"

Stunned, I didn't say anything for a moment while I digested the news by degrees. First, I tried to adjust to the name change. Francis was Harold. Harold was in the hospital. Harold was my friend. Of course I wanted to go see him! I'd been in the hospital once, two years ago when I had my appendix removed. I was only there for two days, but it had seemed like an eternity, and what had cheered me the most was when Sydney's mom brought her to visit.

I'd been focused on my own disappointment all day, but what about Francis—er, Harold? Despite everything, I knew the joy he'd expressed during our training sessions had been genuine, even if everything else he'd said was suspect. Plus, I knew in my heart that he'd been looking forward to today as much or more than Liam and I had. If he really was in bad shape, as Alice had said, he'd definitely be in need of some cheering. I glanced down at Bernard and his sweet face. It might take all three of us—Bernard, Liam, and me—to do the trick. But my parents were away and my only option for a ride was . . . Emma.

"You have a baby sister, right?" I asked Liam.

"Yes," Liam said. He looked confused.

"So you probably have a stroller, too."

"Yes," Liam said, and looked even more confused.

"Great!" I said. "Go grab it and come right back. I'll work on getting us a ride to the hospital."

"But—"

"I'll explain on the way there. Just go!"

Liam dashed out the front entrance, and I took a deep breath, steeling myself. Next, I made a quick stop by my room to grab my finished art project, then carried the frame with me down the hall. I'd been waiting for the perfect moment to give it to my stepsister. But now would have to do. I knocked once. When Emma didn't answer, I knocked again.

"Go away!" she growled.

"Please, Emma." I leaned close to the door. "It's important." When she didn't respond, I gently turned the knob and pushed. Emma was standing next to her dresser. She'd put back all the items Bernard had cleared from it. All except for the broken frame. A photo of Emma and a gray-haired woman was propped against the wall in its place. I stayed light on my feet in case she started throwing things again.

"What do you want?" she said. Then her angry gaze traveled to the frame in my hands.

Before I lost my nerve, I blurted out, "I have a peace offering and . . . a favor to ask. I think you lost someone close to you, right? Your grandmother, maybe?" I glanced at the free-standing photo. The day Emma moved in, she'd said something like "with Grams gone" that her mom saw no reason to stay.

"The frame Bernard broke, it was from your grand-mother, wasn't it?" I asked gently.

Emotion flooded Emma's eyes, her entire face really. Her jaw trembled almost imperceptibly. "Yes," she said.

"I'm *really* sorry," I said. I held the frame out to her. "I know this can't replace the one you lost, but I want you to have it." The neutral colors of the frame gave it an antiqued look. Even Sydney had seemed to admire it more than her own purple-and-blue one. I knew the frame couldn't possibly be as meaningful (coming from me) as the one that broke, but it wasn't like I was offering her a piece of junk or anything.

Still, Emma didn't move to take it.

I tried a different approach. "I'm worried about my friend. His name is . . . Harold. He lives at the retirement community down the street. I was hoping you might give me and Liam a ride to the hospital to visit him."

"Sounds like a *you* problem, not a *me* problem," Emma said huffily, and turned away from me.

"Please?" I begged. "He's old, and I think he's really sick."

Emma stiffened at my words but didn't swivel toward me. "Leave," she said. There was a note of finality in her voice that left no room for discussion.

Even though I was terribly disappointed, I placed the frame on the corner of her dresser. "I want you to have this anyway," I said. "I'm sure it was really hard losing your grandmother and having your mom move away. I guess I can understand why you don't like me. Mom and I butted into your life, and everything changed for you, kinda suddenly." I paused. "Change is hard," I whispered more to myself than to her. Then I quietly slipped out of her room.

Bernard and I waited on the front porch, me scratching his belly, until Liam came pushing a deluxe stroller down the side-walk. It was the perfect stroller for what I had in mind—one with a broad base and a large retractable sun cover. Too bad we wouldn't be able to use it.

The smile on Liam's face fell when he saw the gloomy expression on my own. "I couldn't get us a ride," I said. "I tried, but my stepsister said no."

"False," a voice said from somewhere over my shoulder. I whipped my head around to find Emma standing at the storm door, eyeing Liam's stroller curiously. "I said 'leave,' but I never said 'no.' Get in the car. I'll grab the kennel."

I hadn't said anything to her about bringing Bernard. But apparently, she'd put two and two together when she'd seen the stroller. I leaped to my feet, startling Bernard, who then buoyed to his hooves. "Really?"

"Go before I change my mind," Emma said with an exasperated roll of her eyes.

Emma's car was cramped with Bernard and his kennel in the far back, Liam with the folded-up stroller in the middle, and my stepsister and me in the front. We bounced and jerked at every turn and stoplight. I mumbled something about "wanting to reach the hospital alive" and that I "didn't want to become a patient either."

Emma shot daggers at me with a sidelong glance.

But we made it. And between Emma, Liam, and me, we were able to heft the squealing pig out of the kennel and into the stroller. Then I pulled the sunshade all the way up, enclosing Bernard. He settled in at once, hunkering down in the soft bedding and falling fast asleep.

My dream of being a therapy pig handler was quickly fading, but right now I was more concerned with how Harold was doing. More than anything, I wanted him to be well. I also wanted to make good on my promise to take a photo of him with Bernard in costume. But the stroller was a snug fit, and there hadn't been enough clearance for the top hat. Maybe it was better this way, I reasoned. The photo would give all of us something to look forward to. We just had to get Harold healthy enough to come home first. We *had* to!

The lady at the front desk of the retirement community

had taught me that there were more people in this world like Sydney. People who only saw a repulsive animal when they looked at Bernard. I didn't want to risk running into another pig hater when we brought him inside the hospital. Plus, I knew that without graduating from the therapy animal program, I wasn't supposed to be bringing him in.

Still, it didn't seem fair. I had read through the requirements. Bernard would be the world's most excellent therapy pig. It wasn't his fault that I was too young to get him into the program by myself and that our best shot at it was now stuck inside a place Bernard wasn't supposed to enter unless he was already certified.

Liam pushed the stroller through the parking lot, up the sidewalk, and through the automatic doors. Emma and I followed close behind. She paused just inside. Her skin blanched, and she blew out a deep breath.

"Are you okay?" I asked.

She faltered. I think my concern surprised her. "Yeah, just the last time I was here . . ." Emma trailed off. "Anyway, do you know what room your friend is in?"

I shook my head.

"We'll try at the front desk."

The hospital was bright and airy, with high ceilings and sporadically placed pieces of art. If it wasn't for all the nervous people packed into the waiting areas, it might've reminded me of a museum. But at least Bernard was quiet and still inside the stroller. No one would ever guess that there wasn't a human baby inside.

"What's your friend's name again?" Emma asked.

"Francis. I mean Harold."

"Harold Francis or Francis Harold?"

"Just Harold."

"Harold what?"

"I don't know."

Emma's eyebrows shot up. "Are you serious? You don't know his last name?" Clearly, she wasn't happy.

"He's a newish friend," I offered. "He helped me train Bernard."

Emma took a minute to compose herself. She looked like she regretted going along with my plan. But at last she said, "Okay," and stepped up to the front desk while I waited a few steps back with Liam and Bernard.

"Hi, could you please tell me if you have any patients named Harold?" I'd never heard her speak so sweetly. I assumed it was a kindness reserved only for people who weren't me.

"Last name?" the young man behind the desk asked.

Emma inhaled. "Yeah, about that . . ." she said. "See, I'm helping my little stepsister and her friend. They're determined to visit one of your patients, but they're children. And you know how kids are—always forgetting important details." She laughed hollowly.

I bristled. At eighteen, she was barely an official adult, and in my opinion, she often acted more childish than I did. But when the man behind the counter glanced my direction, I lifted my hands in a shrug and smiled sheepishly.

He seemed to take a moment to contemplate my and Liam's appearance. There was hardly anything menacing about us—two adolescents and a baby carriage. Then his hands hit the keyboard while he stared at the screen. "We have two Harolds. One on the third floor and one in ICU. Does he know you're coming?"

Emma shook her head.

The man picked up a receiver behind the desk. He cupped his hand over the bottom speaker. "What are your names?" he whispered to Emma.

"I'm Emma. That's Grace and Liam," she said.

The man spoke into the receiver. "Hi, yes. Is this Harold?" He paused. "I have an Emma, a Grace, and a Liam here to see you."

"Great. I'll send them up." The man hung up the phone. "Go down the hall. Take the elevator on the right to the third floor. He's in room 312."

"Thank you!" I gushed loudly as Emma moved to usher us away.

Liam rolled the baby carriage right down the hall and into an empty elevator. Emma hit the button and the number 3 illuminated in orange. We were on our way!

Once the elevator swung open, we followed the signs to room 312 and found the door open. The name Harold Longfield was written on a dry-erase board. As we strolled right in, I thought, *This is almost too easy.*

A stranger with brown skin and a gray stubble flashed a megawatt smile at us from his hospital bed as we walked in. I stopped in my tracks. Emma's triumphant expression changed when she saw the look on my face. "I'm guessing this isn't your Harold."

"No," I said, trying for the sake of the man in the hospital bed not to sound as disappointed as I felt.

"Hi there, you must be Emma, Liam, and Grace," Harold Longfield said. "I can't tell you how excited I am to have visitors! Did Shanice send you?"

We found out Harold's family all lived in another state and he'd been complaining to his sister earlier in the day. He assumed we were friends of hers. "Sorry," I apologized. "We thought you were someone else."

"Well, I'm not sorry," Harold said. "It's nice to talk to someone who isn't here to poke me with a needle or take my temperature. Now who's this little one in the carriage?"

"Uh, this is Bernard, my pet pig," I said.

"Nah, you gotta be pulling my leg."

"No, really," I said, and I whipped back the sunshade.

"Well, holy smoke, this just keeps getting better," he said with a laugh.

Bernard woke with a start and grunted loudly. He calmed down at once when he saw Harold peering down at him. His lips curled into an almost smile, and his eyes seemed to sparkle.

"I think the pig likes me," Harold said. I showed him how to scratch Bernard's belly. He seemed to enjoy it so much that we stayed a few minutes longer before continuing on our quest to find the other Harold.

As soon as we left the hospital room, I repositioned the sunshade so Bernard was again hidden from view.

"If that wasn't him," Emma said, "then your Harold must be the one in ICU." She grimaced.

"Is that bad?" I asked.

"ICU stands for intensive care unit," Emma said. "It means that whatever he's here for . . . it's serious."

My stomach fell. Poor Harold. "All the more reason to hurry," I said. "Come on."

"I don't know, Grace. Maybe we shouldn't . . ." Emma dragged her feet as Liam and I bolted forward.

I stopped and turned to face her. "You saw how happy

Bernard made this Harold," I said. "We have to see him. We have to at least try!"

She groaned but quickly relented. "Okay," she said. "We'll give it a shot."

We found a map of the hospital, then rode the elevator down one level to the second floor. As soon as we stepped off, it was obvious that this area of the hospital was different. There wasn't the chatter and energy of the other floors, a set of double doors blocked our path, and even the lights seemed harsher.

"May I help you?" a stern woman called out from behind a desk.

"We're here to see Harold," I said, hoping she wouldn't ask for a last name and would simply provide a room number.

The woman flashed me a strained smile as her eyes drifted to the carriage and then back to me. "I'm sorry, that's not possible. We don't allow infants to visit patients in the ICU."

It took me a moment to realize she was talking about Bernard. Still, if they didn't allow infants, I highly doubted that they would allow pigs. I didn't have a chance to even think about arguing my case before a second woman stepped off the elevator behind us. She was elderly and wearing thick glasses.

"Oh my, a baby!" the woman said delightedly. "You don't mind if I have a peek, do you?" Not waiting for an answer, the woman rolled back the sunshade. She leaned in close. I could see her eyelids fluttering behind the thick lenses. She wrinkled her nose. "Why, he's, um . . . wow . . . He's, um . . . well, he has nice pink skin." The woman seemed distressed by the situation, and I didn't understand why. "Don't fret about the hair," she said to Emma. "My cousin's baby was born with thin, soft hair on her face, too. It disappeared before she turned one, and now she's a stunningly beautiful child."

My eyes widened, and I peered in to see Bernard snuggled into a blanket so that only his eyelids and his pink hairy forehead were visible. The woman with her poor vision must've mistaken him for a human child. No wonder she had struggled so hard to find something nice to say. He was a good-looking pig but a terribly ugly baby.

"Oh," I said, suppressing a giggle. "Um, yes, thank you."

Unfortunately, Bernard chose that moment to pop his eyes open. Finding a stranger in front of him, he grunted deeply and wriggled his snout out from the covers. Obviously startled, the woman let out a bloodcurdling scream, and Bernard shed the blanket entirely and revealed himself for the handsome hog that he was.

18

LiLou, the world's first airport therapy pig, eases the anxieties of travelers at the San Francisco airport.

The chaos that ensued was dizzying. The woman behind the counter was immediately on the phone, calling for security. Emma tried to placate her while Liam tried to comfort the elderly woman, and I shushed Bernard, who was rather upset to have been woken from his nap for no good reason.

In no time, a security guard was there to escort us directly out of the hospital, and no matter how much I begged and pleaded, he wouldn't let us turn around to visit Harold in the ICU. Not even for a minute.

It must've been quite a sight to see. At that point, Bernard was fully exposed to everyone we passed. He let out a stream of happy little snorts and oinks as people rose to their feet and gawked at the pig joyously riding through the hospital in a stroller, then at the teenager, two adolescents, and a beefy guard accompanying him.

The security guard stoically ignored our protests the entire way. But once we stepped outside the front entrance and were standing on the pavement, he cracked a smile. "That's some pig," he said.

"Better than Wilbur," Emma remarked curtly.

"Don't get me wrong," the security guard said. "I'm not against you bringing a pig in to visit patients, but you've got to do it the right way. None of this sneaking-him-in-a-baby-carriage nonsense."

"There's a right way?" Emma asked.

"Why, sure, we have therapy animals making rounds all the time. Animals reduce pain and anxiety, and help people heal."

"Of course!" Emma said. "A therapy dog visited my grandmother while she was in the hospital. Grams was so excited to tell me about it." Her eyes misted. "I just didn't realize that pigs were allowed to, you know, visit patients, too."

I offered her a sad smile and wondered if the therapy dog that had visited her grandmother had something to do with why she'd caved and agreed to help. "Only if one of the handlers is an adult," I said quietly. "But that's true for all therapy animals. Not just pigs."

Emma eyed me curiously as the security guard went on, "I don't see why your pig here couldn't get certified. But he does have to be certified. The hospital has stringent rules. We must be sure the animal is not only trained but also vaccinated and screened for behavior issues. The safety of our patients is our primary concern."

"What all is involved in getting an animal certified?" Emma asked. Now it was my turn to glance at *her* curiously. Was it possible that she was actually interested in the program?

"I'm no expert on the topic, but I know it takes about six months of classes followed by a test."

My shoulders slumped at the reminder. Forget that I wasn't an adult. Even if by some miracle Emma was interested, it would still be a minimum of six months before I could bring Bernard inside the hospital. It made me terribly anxious to think of Harold stuck inside, and us stuck out here, unable to visit. I felt so helpless. The only thing I could do was pray that he'd be all right.

We thanked the security guard and left. Emma drove a thousand times slower than normal, and not even Bernard made a sound during the car ride. We dropped Liam and his stroller off at his house and continued home. After Emma pulled into the driveway and turned off the ignition, we both just sat there.

"I'll do it with you," she said. "I'm eighteen. I can be the adult handler. We can take the classes together. Get Bernard certified as a therapy animal."

As thrilling as this news was, it wasn't enough to drag me completely out of the dumps. "Really?" I asked, not quite able to believe that she meant it. At the same time, Bernard snorted his approval from the back of the car. When Emma and I both turned to look, he bobbed his head and his lips were curled in a smile.

That's what finally broke the cage of gloom I'd been stuck in since that morning. I felt lighter. Happier. That's what Bernard did for people.

Emma's face was bright, too, and I knew Bernard had finally gotten through to her as well. I met her eyes. "Really?" I asked a second time. Because the answer meant more than just a six-month program and a test, and all that came with being therapy pig handlers. It also meant the two of us working together. It meant a commitment to each other, and to Bernard. It meant that she would have to help me convince Mom and Mr. Pine to forget about the trial period and welcome Bernard into our family for good.

Emma held my stare. "Yes," she said. "We probably can't get it done quickly enough to visit your friend—I'm sorry about that. But did you see how happy he made the other Harold?" Emma smiled wistfully to herself. "My grandma would've gone absolutely bonkers for that pig. I think . . . well . . . I think if she had met him, he might've eased some of her suffering, even if it was only by a little." She took her eyes off me and looked up through the windshield, her gaze falling somewhere in the clouds. "Might even make her happier now. So yeah . . . I'm in if you are."

For a moment, I didn't know what to say. I'd never seen this calmer, gentler side of my stepsister. Of course, for as long as I'd known her, she'd been dealing with a great deal of grief and heartache. It'd come up at our parents' wedding—how her grandmother was ill and not expected to live much longer. Then her mom ran off to another state without her. I guess that probably had a big effect on her mood. It would make me sulky and snappy, too.

Even if Bernard couldn't cheer Harold up, there were other people he could. He'd had a huge impact on my life. Not only did I want to keep him forever, I wanted to share him with people who needed a smile. "One hundred percent," I answered. "Thank you."

Mom and Mr. Pine came home the next day, tan and blissfully happy. When they walked in the front door, Emma and I were both snuggling Bernard and watching the movie *Babe* together. It was an older movie that came out before either of us was born about a pig who learned to do the work of a sheepdog.

We both agreed that Bernard and Babe were kindred spirits.

My heart began to race when I made eye contact with Mom. Then I watched breathlessly as she took it all in—me, Bernard, and Emma together in the same room, clearly enjoying one another's company. Mom's eyes grew rounder, and her brows lifted ever so slightly. The corners of her mouth tugged upward. I could tell she'd been affected by the sight. And in that moment, I knew, I just knew, the matter of the trial period had been put to rest.

Relief poured out of me in one giant release of air, and then I felt the broadest smile stretch across my face. For all my fear and worry, when it came down to it, I didn't need a costume or a certification to prove that Bernard was a wonderful pig. It was enough for Mom to see that he had brought me and my stepsister closer together.

Mr. Pine was struggling to drag luggage through the door, and Mom gently elbowed him to get his attention. "Sweetheart," she said, and then she tipped her head toward Emma and me. We were both grinning now while we scratched Bernard behind the ears.

"What?" Mr. Pine asked, clearly still oblivious to the situation.

"That," Mom said, and tipped her head again. "It appears the girls, *and* the pig, bonded while we were away."

"Oh?" my stepdad said. A second later, it seemed to hit him. "Oooh," he repeated himself. Then he half winced, half smiled.

. . .

On Monday, Liam sat at our lunch table again. Sydney did not. But she kept shooting furtive glances our way. I shot a few in her direction, too. I missed her. After being friends for so long, it was like I'd lost a part of myself.

Liam and I caught Alejandra and Jana up on everything that had happened after they had left the retirement community on Saturday. "Do you think Harold lied to us about more than just his name?" Liam asked.

I'd been thinking about that. "I'm not sure," I said honestly. "But I think what he was doing was more like pretending than lying."

"What do you mean?" Liam asked.

"You said he was lonely when you first met him, right?"

"Really lonely."

"Well, what if he was pretending to have had interesting jobs so that we'd think *he* was interesting and would keep coming back to see him."

"That sounds a lot like lying to me," Alejandra interjected.

"Maybe you're right," I said. "But I think he would've told us the truth eventually. Besides, everyone pretends sometimes to make people like them more. I think I pretended all the time I was someone I wasn't when I was around Sydney." That last part slipped out of my mouth before I had a chance to think better of it. It made me nervous to share something so personal. But I didn't take it back. I finally understood that I'd been lying to myself for years. The person I was with Sydney had never been the real me. But I wanted to be myself with everyone from this point forward.

"And, Jana," I went on, "you told me you wear a ton of makeup and fix your hair all fancy for dance recitals. When you're onstage, does it feel like, I don't know, the real you?"

"No," Jana said. "It doesn't. It's like an illusion. But the audience knows that, too. It's the same as it is for the play."

"So maybe it's okay if everyone is in on the secret," I said, thinking aloud. "And Harold called me and Liam by the wrong names from the start. So maybe he was trying to tell us from the very beginning that some of what he said was make-believe."

Liam shrugged. "I guess. I kinda wondered all along if he was just bluffing with those stories."

"I did, too," I said. "I'm not angry with him. But I'd like to have the chance to ask him about it. I'm still really worried about him."

"Yeah," Liam said. "Me too."

After school, Emma met me in the drop-off circle in front of the building. She handed over Bernard's leash, and I walked my pig back inside to practice for the play. Bernard created quite a stir in the halls, but by now, that was nothing new to us.

We bumped into Sydney along the way, and her jaw nearly hit the floor. "So *this* is your pig?" she said. "He's not as repulsive as I thought."

I decided to take that as a compliment. "Um, thanks," I said.

Sydney changed directions and joined me and Bernard as we continued down the hallway. A few steps in, she looped her arm through mine like she had a thousand times before. It felt so comfortable and familiar. Until she started glancing around us, and I realized she was embarrassed to be walking with me and Bernard. We were drawing too much of the wrong kind of attention for her liking. The first corner we came to, she redirected us down an emptier hallway. "I miss you, Grace." She pouted.

"I miss you, too," I said, and my heart panged in a way that I knew the statement was true.

"Look, I'm sorry you couldn't have a real dog. But I guess it's fine if you have a pig," she said.

I bristled. The longing in my heart for how things used to be distorted into something else. Something harder. I didn't need Sydney to approve of my pet. And honestly, I wasn't sorry

Bernard wasn't a dog. Not anymore. I glanced back at him trailing behind us—his flat snout in the air, sucking in whiffs of middle-school air as his tiny hooves pitter-pattered on the tile floor. I was utterly smitten with the animal. And if she couldn't appreciate his many finer qualities, well, that was her problem.

"And Alejandra and Jana are superb. It's totally fine with me if you want to hang out with them more often."

"Okay," I said, but she obviously didn't detect the sharp edge to my voice.

"Plus, Jana, like, needs Bernard for the play. I get it. It makes sense that the two of you would talk more. I didn't mean to get jealous before. But you're *my* best friend."

I stopped walking and stood stone still. Bernard happily drove his nose beneath the row of lockers and investigated what I could only assume was a most intriguing odor. "What about Liam?" I asked.

Sydney balked. "What about him?"

"He's my friend, too."

"Oh, Grace, our lunch table is getting a little crowded, don't you think?"

It hit me that I had two choices. I could pretend I was okay with everything Sydney had just said—with how she continued to belittle me and Bernard and sought to drive me and Liam apart. That was the path to restoring our friendship. Or I could walk away. I was reminded of the lunch table conversation earlier that day about the difference between lying and pretending. And I decided that for something to be a lie, you had to know what you were saying or doing was wrong and choose to do it anyway.

I'd pretended I was someone I wasn't before to remain Sydney's friend. But now, if I chose her, it would be a lie. Not only that, it would mean giving up Liam, and Liam had never once made me feel small or unimportant. He'd never done anything to make me feel less than—not in the slightest. I didn't care if he wore the wrong clothes, had unruly hair, and geeked out over insects or whatever else—what we had was true. What I had with Sydney wasn't.

I peeled her arm off mine. "Sydney," I said. "I like our lunch table the way it is now. If you want to sit with us, that's your choice. But we're not asking anyone to leave."

Sydney clucked her tongue. "Seriously, Grace, you're going to choose Liam Rossi over me?"

I held my ground. "Yes, Sydney, I am," I said.

She exuded a loud, disgusting noise, like she was clearing phlegm from her throat, and Bernard snapped to attention. He snorted gleefully, like he was thinking, *Finally someone is speaking my language.*

Sydney was wearing knee socks and a skirt, and Bernard

planted his snout against the bare-skinned crook of her left knee. Her eyes widened. Her cheeks ballooned, and she turned a light shade of green. She looked like she was about to vomit before she stormed off. After she was gone, I bent over and drew Bernard into a hug. "Good pig," I said. "Good, good pig." Then I told him to come, and the two of us continued to make our way toward the theater.

Jana greeted us at the double doors, bubbling with nervous energy. "There you are!"

I smiled at her reassuringly before handing over Bernard's leash. "Don't worry, you'll both do great," I said. Then I gave Jana a few Cheerios to stick in her pocket and headed off to find a place to hang out in the wings. Sure enough, Bernard followed her around like a lost puppy onstage. He was a natural—they both were. And I was thankful for the opportunity for him to be around so many new people. Not that strangers seemed to bother him any these days. He'd come so far from the wary pig he'd been on Christmas morning.

After theater practice, Emma was standing by her car in front of the school building. I'd been expecting Mom and I felt a wave a disappointment, thinking she'd been suddenly called away on another business trip. But that wasn't the case. Apparently, Emma had volunteered to pick me and Bernard up because she couldn't wait to tell us the good news. She'd enrolled the three of us in a therapy animal certification program. We could start classes almost immediately.

Even though I had no regrets about the way things had ended with Sydney, my heart had felt heavy in my chest ever since. This was exactly what I needed. I rushed to Emma. I wrapped my arms around my stepsister and squeezed her tight. She stiffened at first, but then she rested her head on top of mine, and she hugged me right back.

19

Pigs have been known to help save human lives. A Vietnamese potbellied pig named LuLu alerted a passerby when her owner had a heart attack. Another potbellied pig, this one named Ludwig, chased away burglars from his family's home.

Emma and I took online courses in the evenings. The classes were about reading the therapy animal's body language as well as safety and welfare considerations for visiting health-care settings. There would be a rigorous test that we'd all have to pass at the end.

Not that I was surprised, but Bernard fit all the criteria. He now loved being around people and showed no signs of aggression. Plus, Harold had prepared him well with all the obedience training we'd done together. Not to mention how Bernard lost his mind over having his belly scratched. Apparently, even that was important—that the animal liked being touched. The only thing that had me concerned was that we'd have to demonstrate his skills for an evaluator, and we still hadn't mastered the "leave it" command.

Between theater practice and therapy animal training, I hardly had time for anything else. Luckily, the art program I attended with Sydney had ended with the completion of the frame. Mom usually scheduled my extracurricular activities weeks in advance and would have the next class all lined up. But it must've slipped her mind while she was on vacation. When I came home right after school on a day that I normally would have art class, she realized her mistake. Of course, Mom assumed I wanted to sign up for another session. "I'll call Sydney's mom right away to coordinate," she said, and headed into the kitchen to retrieve her cell phone from the counter. "I bet it's not too late."

"No!" I answered a bit too forcefully as I trailed behind her.

Mom set her phone back down and studied my face. "What's going on?"

I hadn't said anything to her about my falling-out with my best friend. I bit my bottom lip. My mom and Sydney's mom had known each other since before either of us was born. "Um," I said, staring at the floor. "I don't really want to take another class with Sydney. She and I aren't close anymore. *But* I am thinking about joining the photography club."

I peeked up to see that Mom's eyebrows were raised. But then a look of understanding settled on her face. She must've recognized something in my eyes, or maybe she'd known all along that Sydney and I were poorly matched. "Yes, of course," she said. "Not every relationship is worth saving."

I nodded, and she went on, "Sometimes people aren't good for each other. Sometimes, they simply grow apart. And that's okay."

I wanted to feel reassured by her words. Instead they hit on one of my deepest fears. We'd made it past Bernard's trial period, and Emma and I were learning to act like sisters on our best days and coexist on the others. (She still thought I was messy, and I still wasn't comfortable with her driving.) Yet, I worried what we had accomplished wasn't enough to keep us all together. I occasionally caught an edge to Mom's voice when she was speaking to my stepdad. And I knew for certain that Bernard and I were an annoyance when my pig tipped over a trash can, or I got too excited about one thing or moody about something else and drew Mom's attention away from Mr. Pine.

I wanted to feel secure, but I didn't. "Mom," I said, "do you ever worry that we're going to grow apart? Not me and you necessarily, but the five of us?" (Of course, I was counting Bernard as part of the family.)

Mom's eyebrows drew together with concern. "Why would you ask that?"

"What happens when Mr. Pine gets sick of my messes

and outbursts? You're so much happier now, and I don't want to screw things up for you. Not again."

"What do you mean, again?" Mom studied my face.

"You know, why Dad left. I wasn't an easy child. Remember?"

Mom closed her eyes and breathed in deeply before opening them and exhaling loudly. "Oh, Grace, you are not the reason your father left. Your father is the reason he left. And you are allowed to be messy and imperfect. I wouldn't want you to be anything other than who you are, and neither would your stepdad."

"How do you know?" I challenged her.

"Because he loves you."

"How do you know?" I asked again.

As she thought, she glanced down. Then she jolted slightly and smiled while plucking a sticky note from the kitchen counter. It had been lying next to her cell phone the entire time, but neither of us had noticed because we'd been lost in conversation. "Well, for one thing—this," she said, and handed me the note.

It read:

Grace,

Emma told me about your friend Harold. I'm really sorry. Come talk to me when you get home from school. I think I can get you and your friend Liam in to see him.

—Nathan

I clutched the note and stared at Mom, dumbfounded, as a warm feeling spread through my chest.

"Yeah," said Mom. "I know because he's one of the good ones. Sometimes we have to go through bad relationships to figure out how to tell them apart. But he isn't going anywhere. He loves us both."

I thanked her and then darted down into the basement to find Mr. Pine. "Can you really?" I asked as soon as I saw him seated at his desk. I was too anxious to be tactful.

"Grace," he said. "You found my note."

"*Yes.*" I bounced on my toes impatiently. "Tell me about Harold."

A smile slowly spread across Mr. Pine's face. "A friend of mine works the night shift at the retirement community. He knows Harold—last name is Bernadone, by the way—and he said your friend suffered a massive heart attack last week."

"Okay," I said. "And?" My breath stopped flowing. I held it locked inside my lungs.

"I called the hospital to inquire about him this morning. They said Harold Bernadone was moved out of the ICU into a regular care unit yesterday. He's doing much better."

I waveringly let out all the air I'd trapped inside. "That's great! Really great," I said. I felt a rush of gratitude toward

Mr. Pine. Maybe Mom was right. Maybe he was one of the good ones.

"He can have visitors now," my stepfather said, then with a quirk of his lips added, "Human ones, at least."

Mr. Pine brought me and Liam to see Harold later that evening. He waited in the hallway outside while Liam and I went in. Harold's eyes were closed. I held back at first. It was unnerving to see him in a gown and with so many tubes and machines surrounding him. I much preferred visiting with him at the retirement community.

But Liam went straight to Harold's bedside. On the way to the hospital, Liam told us that he'd visited his mom here when each of his six siblings were born. Maybe the more times you visited a hospital, the less overwhelming it felt. I hoped that was the case considering I planned to spend a great deal of time visiting patients here with Bernard and Emma in the near future.

Sure enough, when Harold opened his eyes and began talking, the uncomfortable feeling melted away. "Well, if isn't Grace and Liam," he said playfully.

"You actually called us by our real names," I noted.

Harold grinned sheepishly. "Did I? Must be all the oxygen they're pumping inside me. Makes my brain work better."

"I think your brain works just fine, with or without extra oxygen," Liam said.

"You might be right about that," Harold said, then patted his chest. "It's my ticker that's giving me so much trouble."

"Why did you tell us your name was Francis?" I asked, getting right to the point. "It made it difficult for us to find you."

"I don't know that I have a good answer for that," Harold admitted. "I guess I thought if you forgot about some old fart named Francis, it wouldn't hurt as badly as if you forgot about me, Harold."

"We'd never forget about you!" I protested.

"Is that so?" Harold smiled wryly. "Maybe it doesn't seem like it now, but most old people are forgettable to the younger generations. It's the way it is, but that doesn't make it any easier to swallow."

"Was everything else you told us a lie, too?" I asked. "All the crazy jobs you said you had—did you make up stories about yourself so we'd keep coming back to see you?"

Harold briefly shut his eyes and sucked in air through the oxygen tube in his nose. When he opened his eyes again, he was smiling a sad, pensive smile. "No, the stories I told you were true, and regrettably they are all that I have to show for myself."

"What does that mean?" Liam asked.

"I never appreciated what was in front of me because I was always preoccupied with finding something better. Do you know that you two are the only visitors I've had?"

I shook my head. "What are you talking about?" I was starting to think the oxygen was affecting his brain—*in a bad way*.

"I was never satisfied. I bounced around the world going from one job to the next. I was chasing frivolous things and leaving behind the people I cared about. What did it get me? Interesting stories, but no one to share them with."

"You shared your stories with us," I said.

"That I did," Harold said, and the whites of his eyes turned glassy. "And to be frank, I was tired and ready to give in—seventy-nine years is a heck of a long time to spend alone—when one of the nurses told me a story about a couple of crazy kids trying to sneak a pig into the ICU in a baby carriage." Harold's eyes were still misty, but he grinned ear to ear and tapped the side of his nose. "I reckoned I knew exactly who those daring culprits were."

Liam and I stared at each other out of the corner of our eyes and smiled.

"It gave me just the boost I needed," said Harold, "knowing there were at least a few kids and a hog who cared whether I lived or died. Doctor said I'll be able to return to the retirement community in a few days."

I breathed an enormous sigh of relief. "That's great news!" I said. "I can't wait for you to see Bernard's costume, and . . . and I have some big news myself. My stepsister and I are taking classes to get Bernard certified as a therapy pig. We'll take him to hospitals and nursing homes and libraries, and all sorts of places, so he can cheer people up. We have to pass an evaluation at the end of the program, but Bernard's acing all his classes thanks to you! His instructor said she's never seen a more obedient pig."

Harold puffed up with pride. "Well, isn't that something? That might be the coolest job I've ever heard of. Makes me want to come out of retirement."

I bit down on one side of my lip, debating if I should tell him that he had been my first choice for co-handler.

"Ah, but those days are behind me," he said. "Besides, I think this is the type of thing that could turn sisters into friends for life." There was an extra twinkle in his eyes, what with all the emotion everyone in the room was feeling.

"I hope so," I said. I'd learned from my therapy animal classes not to stay too long. Hospital patients need company, but they also need lots of rest. "There is one thing you might be able to help me with before we go? No matter what I try, I can't get Bernard to listen when I tell him to 'leave it.'"

Harold grinned, and I could tell he liked feeling needed. We left shortly after he gave me a few helpful pointers, and Mr. Pine was waiting for me and Liam right outside the door. I may not have agreed with all my stepdad's choices—certainly not his taste in ice cream. And I knew there were things about imperfect me that frustrated him, too. But Mr. Pine was firmly in my corner when it counted. We were family, through thick and thin.

I met his gaze with my own. "Thank you, M—" I stopped myself. "Thank you, Nathan," I said, because I still wasn't comfortable with calling him "Dad," but his first name felt like a step in the right direction.

You would've thought he'd won the lottery as brightly as he beamed back at me.

. . .

Six weeks later, Bernard stole the show at the Riverbend Middle School production of *The Princess and the Pauper*. Alejandra, Liam, and I had front-row seats. For all the practices and the dress rehearsal, Jana had pretended to sell fake flowers. Bernard hadn't shown much interest in the plastic petals and stems. The fresh roses Jana held on opening night were another story.

Unbeknownst to Jana, but visible to everyone else, Bernard stripped rose petals one by one from the entire bouquet while she held it behind her back. The look of shock on her face when she whipped them around and tried to peddle nothing but thorny stems was priceless. Laughter rippled through the audience. It grew louder when Bernard decided rose petals didn't agree with his palate, and he spit them out on the stage.

Fortunately, Jana was as comfortable in the limelight as anywhere else, and she recovered quickly. She tossed the empty stems aside, performed an impromptu pirouette, and asked for payment for her performance instead of the roses.

As I chuckled along with the crowd, I felt Liam's pinkie finger connect with the bare skin of my right hand on our shared armrest. My breath hitched. A zing ran through me. When I didn't pull away, he slowly laced his fingers through mine. We held hands for the remainder of the play. Luckily, the lights were dimmed so he couldn't see me blush.

Emma, Bernard, and I continued taking classes through the spring and into the summer. Mom even broke down and bought me a cell phone so I could film the skills we worked on to submit to the instructor. It took a ton of practice, but Harold's advice on teaching Bernard the "leave it" skill paid off. It boiled down to me anticipating when Bernard was going to be interested in something he shouldn't have. Instead of telling him to "leave it" when he was right on top of an object he found intriguing, I worked on backing him away by stepping in front of him and then lavishing him with praise before he ever reached it. Once he got the hang of backing away on command, it was only a small leap to getting him to "leave it" every time. He performed the trick flawlessly on the video clip I sent.

The cell phone came in very handy for the classes, but the Polaroid camera was still my go-to for taking portraits. When Harold had returned from the hospital a few days after we'd visited him there, I'd marched Bernard, dressed in his top hat and cape of course, down to the retirement community for the photo shoot. When Harold saw Bernard, happy tears sprang from his eyes, and I'm proud to say I captured the joyous reunion, snapping photo after photo with my camera. The way the images seemed to magically appear on the film helped spread smiles more readily than a digital camera ever could. Needless to say, everyone in the photography club loved them.

When the day of the evaluation finally rolled around, I was super nervous. All the classes had been online, but to receive the official certification we had to bring Bernard to the training center to demonstrate his skills.

He had to walk obediently on a leash and show how he wasn't bothered by people petting him or things that he might be exposed to in various environments, like angry yelling and crowds. Then the evaluators rolled by in wheelchairs and clattered behind us with walkers to be certain he wouldn't be easily spooked by either of those things. Fortunately, as much time as he'd spent in the gardens of the retirement community, walkers and wheelchairs were nearly as familiar to him as his favorite blanket.

It was only when the evaluator tested Bernard by dropping a pill case right in front of him that I experienced a moment of panic. Bernard's snout snapped to life, and he looked ready to pounce. But when I stepped in front of him and resolutely commanded him to "leave it," he obediently backed away. I don't know why I'd been worried. He passed the entire evaluation with flying colors, and so did his handlers. We were officially cleared to spread as much joy and cheer as possible.

To celebrate our accomplishment, Liam and Harold organized a graduation party at the retirement community. They tied helium balloons to the fence posts and hung streamers around the garden. There were plenty of blueberry muffins and punch to go around.

Mom and Nathan came, and so did Alejandra and Jana and a few of Emma's friends. Alice was there with her hot pink walker, along with most of the other residents. Jana's mom had sewn sequins onto Bernard's black cape while we were taking the exam. It now read "Bernard the Therapy Pig!" in sparkly red letters. Liam ran the photo booth, and Alejandra set up a "Feed the Pig" stand that was really a beanbag toss featuring a painted pig with a hole for a mouth.

While I was telling Alice all about the test, Nathan walked by and gave my arm a light squeeze. "That's one proud dad you have," Alice commented once he was out of earshot.

Not long ago I would've felt the need to clarify that he was my "stepdad." I didn't feel that now. "Yes," I said. "Thank you."

As I wandered around and mingled with the guests, I was so happy I thought I might explode. This was far from what I'd imagined pet ownership would be like. It surprised me how different it was from the perfect life I'd imagined with the perfect dog.

Instead, I had a pig. A wonderful pig. He wasn't perfect, though. Despite his training, he'd still overturn trash cans and wreak havoc in the house if we didn't keep a close eye on him. But I wasn't perfect either. And that was okay. I'd learned from Harold that if you spent too much time chasing the wrong things, you'd miss out on other things that were even more amazing.

My family was never going to have the best Christmas photo. We'd never be the best-looking family, have the largest home, or go on the fanciest vacations. But so what if my life would never be *picture* perfect? It was even better. It was *pig*ture perfect.

About the Author

Jenny Goebel is the author of *Grave Images*, The 39 Clues: *Mission Hurricane*, *Fortune Falls*, *Out of My Shell*, and *Alpaca My Bags*. She lives in Denver with her husband and three sons. She can be found online at jennygoebel.com.